ALMOST THE SAME BLUE
AND OTHER STORIES

John O'Donnell

Doire Press

First published in 2020

Doire Press
Aille, Inverin
Co. Galway
www.doirepress.com

Layout: Lisa Frank
Cover design: Tríona Walsh
Cover art: Michelene Huggard
Author photo: John Minihan

Printed by Clódóirí CL
Casla, Co. na Gaillimhe

ISBN 978-1-907682-75-9

We gratefully acknowledge the support and assistance of The Arts Council of Ireland.

In memory of Mary O'Donnell (1933 - 2015)
and Barry O'Donnell (1926 - 2019)

CONTENTS

We do not really mean that what we are about to say is true. A story, a story; let it come, let it go.

— from the Ashanti

MARKS

She's standing over me and I can smell ThreeNines off her, his cheap cigars, the faint whiff of Old Spice. 'Get up,' she says, 'get up, Con.' 'Leave me be, Ma,' I say to her, turning over, but she whips the duvet off me and suddenly it's Baltic. 'Get up, would you,' she says, 'your lift's downstairs.' That'll be Hoppy, with the Skoda parked outside, no doubt: I can hear him in the hallway, smarming up to my little sister. 'Fifth Year, is it? I thought you'd finished school.' Siobhan is buying it as well, smirking at him as she chews her hair in a way she doesn't know is lovely. 'There you are,' says Hoppy, looking up at me as I'm barrelling down towards the front door, still buttoning my shirt. 'We're off so, Mrs Kearney,' he says to the old doll, before turning to my sister. 'Bye, Siobhan,' he says, flashing her a grin, his teeth a row of crooked tombstones. 'Bye, Hoppy,' says Siobhan, smiling back.

'You'd better have it for me later,' Hoppy says to me, 'or I won't be responsible.' The interior of the Skoda is grimly pristine, like that room in *Silent Witness* where your one cuts up the stiffs. *Next Turn Garth Brooks Plaza* says the road-sign. Hoppy veers left and the white roof rises up ahead of us, a giant Stetson. I've no chance of finding a monkey for him by tonight, and Hoppy knows it. The old doll's not got it, nor Siobhan neither; and even if they had they wouldn't give it to me, not after the row about Siobhan's babysitting money going missing from the *Toy Story* DVD. 'I already told you,' I said to them, Siobhan bawling her eyes out and the old doll waving the empty plastic DVD case in my face, 'I don't have your stupid money.' I didn't have it either, not by then: Doncaster, 3.30, *Compagnero*, 8 to 1, and for all I know it's out there still, or else it's sliced and diced and stewed in its own juices in some tin. Like I'll be if I don't get Hoppy back his money. Because that pair he kicks around with, they don't mess about. The Twins.

Oh sure, I could tell ThreeNines. Tom Nyhan, Sergeant; NyhanNyhanNyhan, some smart-arse called him, and ThreeNines now, for short. My old doll's squeeze these last two years. He knows I hate him. He'd lean on the counter in the station and wink back at Kennedy, the other blue: 'D'you hear that, Kenno? Dolores's young fella owes Aidan Hopkins five hundred.' The way he says the old doll's name; I can't stand it. 'For the ponies. And now Hopkins is saying if he doesn't get it back this evening, he'll have young Con here done for.' Kennedy, the little scut that he is, would be smirking and rolling his eyes to heaven inside in the office. 'I've packed it in,' I'd want to say then, 'I've packed it in and I'm never having another bet, so fuck the pair of ye.' And I'd walk out, leaving the both of them sniggering behind me. With the €4.30 I have left still in my pocket.

Way back before it became Boylesports it was Meaney's. 'The best name for a bookie yet,' my father'd say as he'd push open the door and we'd step in. 'Howiya, Ram,' Fonsie Meaney'd say to my father, watching as he thumbed over the notes. Then, the first time that he tossed a stray fiver in my direction: 'Try this,' he said: Navan, 4.15, *Just Kidding*, 6 to 1. I could feel their eyes on me as I filled out the docket: Fonsie, and my father, and Higgins, the solicitor's apprentice with his arse propped up against the wall. When I walked over to the counter it was like being on parade. He was beaten a short head. 'Wuh-hoh!' said Higgins, who'd backed the winner, or was letting on he had anyway. But by then they had me, and they knew it. The bays and chestnuts, the candy-coloured silks, hunched and steering, the flying clumps of kicked-up turf and the screeching of the commentator, rising in excitement; and the rising up inside of me as well, where winning was the best, but nearly winning was nearly as good, was almost better, because of the win that was certain to come next. 'We'll have to put a block on young Con's head to stop him growing,' Fonsie'd say each time I was in there after that, until I grew tall enough to look him in the eye, although I never did, not even after my father died, and sometimes I wished they'd tied a block around my ankles, to stop me going in.

But I'm finished with all that now. A mug's game, I keep repeating to myself, the way they tell you to; never again. And anyway, €4.30: there's no longshot would've got me out with Hoppy on that, not even up in Boylesports. So how much damage could those two gorillas do to me, I'm wondering as we head in the back-door of the Plaza to get changed, and then I think of MacNamee, barely breathing when the blues found him at the bottom of the quarry, and I start praying that Roz has put me on Till 6. Because that's my only chance.

The roster's up already, and Roz's neatly looping hand says I'm on Till 5. I'm doing up my tunic when she comes waddling towards us, carrying her clipboard. 'Anyone seen Mac?' she asks. Silence at first: *does she not know about the quarry?* 'Sure he's above in hospital,' Hoppy says eventually. Roz's foot taps out a tiny drum tattoo. 'Ok, so,' she says in her Shift-Leader voice, 'you do 6 today, Aidan. Con, you do… actually, no. Con, *you* do 6. Aidan, you're on 5.' *Winner alright, winner alright*, the fuzzy tannoy in my head is saying; and maybe after all there is a God.

The best marks are the young lads, especially if they're with a young one; they're so busy showing off they hardly ever check. Palm the twenty, turn away, ring up ten. *Oh no, sir, definitely a ten. Here's the print-out, sir; and look.* You hit the return key with a flourish, and the drawer springs open, showing the stacks of tenners and not a single twenty. One old dame nearly snares me, shaking her head and peering into the till as the queue shuffles restlessly behind her. 'This isn't right,' she witters as she turns away eventually. But Till 6 is just outside the CCTV's range, so there's no way Roz can see even if someone complains. By first break I've €100; by lunch break I've €360. The Plaza's humming. They roll in off the motorway, pasty-faced, exhausted; you could serve them up the leg of the Lamb of God and they wouldn't notice. At his break Hoppy is leaning over one of the banquettes talking to The Twins. He points in my direction as the two of them stuff their faces; one of them has a splotch of dark-red burger sauce on his uniform. *Storm Security*, their black jackets say, and there's a big bolt of lightning high up on each sleeve. They're not even brothers, although that's no consolation to MacNamee stretched out above in Intensive Care after the trimming that everybody's saying was from the pair of them. 'See you in Queally's, Hoppy,' I say, real friendly, as I pass him on my way for my own break. But Hoppy just says nothing, and later on the Skoda wheelspins out of the carpark. The afternoon is quieter, but they still come piling in and I still keep piling them up, those beautiful twenties the colour of a summer sky stashed inside my pocket. By clock-off I've €540, and I walk the mile of road back into town. Because before I go to Queally's there's something that I need to do.

I push the door. The place is tumbleweed; the only other punter is Higgins, thinning now on top, in his plum suit and scuffed shoes. 'Any luck?' I say. 'Cartoons,' he says, nodding at the virtual racing on the screens. I pass the pinned-up pages from *The Sporting Life*, and the sheaf of dockets; I take a twenty out and walk up to the counter. 'Hi Aoife,' I say into the glass. And for the first time today I smile. Aoife Meaney: she's with MacNamee, but there's something in those hazel eyes that makes my own eyes water, always has. 'Hi Con,' she says, smiling. She has a bruise over her left eyebrow that she's tried to hide with make-up. 'For Rubin,' I say, pushing over the twenty. Her son; he's special needs, and it's his birthday tomorrow. 'Awh, Con. Thanks,' she says. She smiles at me again, a real big smile this time. 'How's Mac?' I say then. She shifts in her seat. 'The same,' she says. She looks away, and for a moment neither of us says anything. 'So,' she says, recovering herself, 'are you having...?' 'No,' I say, real proud, 'no bet.' I turn to leave, and then look over my shoulder. 'Maybe see you in Queally's later?' I say, and she grins back. 'Yeah,' she says, 'maybe.'

I've the door pulled open, and I'm half out on the footpath when a car goes up the street: the Skoda, with Siobhan in the back; still in her school uniform, it looks like, and someone else in there beside her. But it isn't Hoppy driving; it's the taller of the two, and I can just about make out the flash of lightning on his sleeve. I'm about to run up after them but the Skoda disappears, leaving the street emptier than before. The door's about to close behind me, but I stop it with my foot. I lean back against it, and it opens a bit more, so I can see inside the bottom corner of one of *The Life*'s pages: Crayford Dogs, 6.52, *Take Your Marks*, 3 to 1. And it's swelling up inside me now once more like organ-music, the feeling that you get when you know your luck is in. I'm in control here, I tell myself as I turn back towards the counter, snatching up a docket and pulling out a fistful of twenties, I'm in total control.

SHELLEY

You said for me to say what happened, so I am, I'm saying it now; nothing happened. I don't care what I said earlier, 'cos this time I'm telling you the truth.

Shelley's twelve. Same as me. Her Mam's Tracey. Tracey and Mam are friends, or were until all this. Tracey's in our house all the time. Darren says she should have her own key.

Shelley's in a different school to me. A special school, Mam says. She's weird. I used to be scared of her. 'It's rude to stare, Jimmy,' Mam kept saying to me but I couldn't help it. Especially when she talked, because Shelley's words came out all muffled, like she was speaking with her mouth full.

When Tracey and Shelley come round, me and Shelley watch videos while Mam and Tracey light up and yack away in the kitchen. She's no good at PlayStation, Shelley. All she ever wants to do is watch DVDs. She loves *Father Ted*.

Father Jack is her favourite. We never go to Shelley's place. Darren says I'm not missing much. He's not the worst, Darren, though he really loses it if Mam's been drinking. Last time there was a huge row, Darren shouting, and Mam crying and telling him he was a bully. He made her promise to give it up then, or he'd leave.

Anyway, this afternoon I'm telling about, Tracey came round with Shelley. It was still school holidays and I was on PlayStation. Tracey looked really posh; heels and lipstick and a tight dress. She kept talking about 'the interview' and asking Mam and me to wish her luck. Mam said the manager would have to be dead from the waist down not to give her the job. They both started giggling and fussing, and then the front door closed and Tracey was gone and it was just Mam and Shelley and me.

We'd watched two episodes when Mam's mobile rang. I could hear Tracey squeaking at the other end. Mam closed her phone and said, 'She's got the job, she's got the job,' and gave us both a hug. Then she looked at Shelley and me. 'Tracey's down in Ryan's having a drink to celebrate,' she said. 'You'll be okay here, the two of you, if I just go down for one drink, won't you?' I turned up the remote a bit and looked over at Shelley, but she didn't look back. Mam went up to change her top and put on some lipstick. 'One drink,' she said, and the door closed and then it was just Shelley and me.

Vodka. I knew where Mam hides it so Darren won't know she's drinking. In the toilet. In a plastic bag at the bottom of the cistern. I lifted up the lid and put my hand down into the water. There was still a good bit left; more than half a bottle. I brought the bottle back to the front room. Mam had given us each some Coke so there were still two glasses on the table in front of the TV. I poured some vodka into my glass and some into Shelley's and I poured some Coke in for each of us. Shelley smiled; her funny crooked smile. Then we both took a drink. It didn't taste any different. I poured some more vodka into both our glasses and we drank again. Then I poured in some more Coke, and more vodka until it was gone and then we drank again.

Father Ted was still on. The milkman one. But Shelley wasn't watching. She kept looking over at me, smiling that stupid smile. Then she moved over beside me, and fell on top of me. She's a ton weight, Shelley, and I wanted to get her off of me, but I was starting to feel a bit blurry and it was kind of nice, her lying on top of me. Then she started to kiss me, all over my face and cheeks and nose and ears. And then my mouth. She stopped and said my name. 'Jibby, Jibby.' Then she started slobbering over me again.

I didn't kiss her back. Not really. She was so heavy I could hardly breathe. I just moved her over slightly. She had her knee in between my legs. She kept squirming around, like she couldn't get comfortable. I could see her legs moving, and her bum. She had on these trackie bottoms; black with three white stripes. She stopped slobbering for a moment, and giggled. Then she started to pull down her trackie bottoms. I swear I didn't do it, and I didn't make her do it. She had these knickers underneath, like swimming togs; white with a little gold star. Then she put her hand inside my trackie. So, yeah, I put my hand inside her knickers; but only for a second. Like I said to that policewoman earlier, before the court case, I touched her. Yeah, *there*. With my finger. Yeah, my first finger. But only for a second. And I didn't put it in. I swear to you I didn't put it in.

She was lying there with her eyes closed. She had her hand inside my trackie, on my privates. I definitely didn't put my privates in. Yeah, I know what my privates are. Definitely I didn't. I felt kind of warm and nice and sleepy, and I took my hand out of her knickers. Then her eyes opened and she took her hand away. She sat up and looked at me, smiling. 'I lubya Jibby,' she said, twice. *I love you Jimmy.* Then her face changed, as if she'd seen something she was afraid of, and she fell off the couch and started to get sick. And at that moment the door opened and Mam and Tracey came in, kind of tottering. Mam saw the sick and asked what happened and Shelley started to cry; only not just an ordinary cry, more a roar. Tracey went to hug her and saw the vodka bottle and Shelley's trackie bottoms on the floor. Then Tracey started roaring. Shelley had big tears coming down her cheeks and she was pointing at me and saying 'Jibby, Jibby.' Then Tracey started hitting me and calling me a bastard and Mam was shouting at Tracey to let go, let go, and I suddenly felt more blurry than ever before and really full up inside of everything, and then I got sick.

I could hear them outside, shouting and banging on the van. 'Little pervert,' one kept saying. 'Ya little pervert.' When we got into the court the lawyers were all standing around like great black birds. Then the judge came out. He had a big red face and tiny little glasses, and he made them all take off their wigs and capes 'because of the age of the accused, and the main witness.' I'd met mine already, at the detention centre. She was okay. She had grey hair, curly at the ends; she looked a bit like that picture of George Washington the teacher showed us once in school.

When Shelley came up to say her story, George Washington jumped up and objected and the jury were sent out. There was a big row between her and Redface, but Redface said Shelley was allowed to give her evidence if she understood the oath. I didn't get this 'giving' bit, or the 'oath,' but then the lawyer on Shelley's side asked her did she know what would happen if she told a lie. He had a gold pen he kept fiddling with while he was asking questions. Shelley said she'd be sent Down Below if she told a lie, but Redface couldn't make out what she said and nor could Goldpen, nor the woman doing the typing, so Tracey had to explain it, and Redface sighed and said proceed.

It was very quiet when Shelley was telling her story to Goldpen. He kept repeating her answers, making it sound worse. People at the back started hissing and giving out when Shelley mentioned the vodka. Goldpen asked about my finger and how long it had been *there*, and Shelley said an hour. Goldpen asked again, and Shelley said a minute.

George Washington turned round and smiled at Mam then, like she'd won something. Goldpen asked about my privates and Shelley said she touched it but that I didn't put it in. Then George Washington got up and started asking all sorts of questions about times of things like TV programmes and classes, and Shelley got all muddled and started to cry. George Washington asked her if she'd been promised anything for coming to the court, and Shelley said her Mam had told her she could have any My Little Pony she wanted if she came here. George Washington glanced back at Mam again, and I could see Tracey's face going all red. Shelley seemed like she was trying not to look at me when she was answering, but she did look once or twice. One time she even waved. 'Hi Jibby,' she said. Then a doctor said some stuff, and a policewoman, and then it was my turn.

I don't know why I lied. I told George Washington when she was asking me what I'd told her before: nothing happened. Then when she was finished with me, Goldpen started asking me loads of questions, and I got really nervous. Goldpen kept twisting my words, so I just kept saying 'no' and 'nothing happened' all the time. I could see George Washington getting flustered and Redface getting redder and redder. He looked at me over the top of his glasses. 'You have to tell the truth, Jimmy,' he said. 'You have to tell the truth'. 'I *am* telling the truth,' I said. Because nothing did happen, really. By the time I was finished one of the jury was shaking his head and Redface was sighing and Goldpen was standing there, smirking and playing with that stupid pen and saying 'Is that the truth, Jimmy? Really?' George Washington wasn't even looking at me anymore; she was looking at Mam. But Mam was just staring, with her mouth open.

The next day, another woman doctor came in to talk about sex and my 'capacity to understand'. Then Goldpen and George Washington each gave a big long lecture to the jury, and Redface gave an even longer lecture. Then the jury went off out of the court. George Washington came over and said 'Well, we've a chance,' and we all just hung around, waiting. After a while I really needed to go to the jacks so I was let go out with a policeman. Shelley was outside, with Tracey and Goldpen. I waved at her but she didn't see me. Then someone came running down the corridor saying 'They're back, they're back.'

When the head of the jury said 'Guilty' there was a big cheer. Tracey was on her feet shouting 'Yes, yes,' and Mam was crying. Redface banged his desk and said this was a courthouse not a public house and started talking about reports and stuff. George Washington got up asking about bail but Redface just looked at me and shook his head and said his options were very limited. That's when I knew, I suppose. That I wasn't going home.

We have classes and art and football here. The food isn't bad. They've given me a new name so no one will know. I'm in a room with two other boys. They don't really talk to me much, though the way one of them looks at me sometimes, I think he knows. There's a lady I see once a month. Maureen. She has this big blue folder and she asks loads of questions and makes loads of notes. She talks about getting out 'on licence' and asks me do I feel 'remorse'. I haven't a clue what she means. So I say 'Yeah, kind of,' and she makes another note. It's full of notes and letters and reports, that folder; there's even a photo of me, when I was ten.

Mam comes every week. She used to cry each time, but now she doesn't. Not in the Visiting Centre, anyway. Her eyes are always red, though, and she looks real thin. I used to cry each time as well, but now it's not so bad. Darren even came a couple of times, at the beginning. But not since. I still miss Mam, though. I even miss Darren.

And sometimes I think of Shelley. Once when Maureen was checking something in one of the reports I saw a page from a school copybook pinned inside the folder. Shelley's writing; it's really, really bad. *Dear Jimmy*, it said. *I hope you are well. I am well. We have a new teacher. I have a new My Little Pony. I love Father Ted. I love you Jimmy. Lots of love, Shelley.* With a big X beside her name. There was some sort of letter from Shelley's school in with it as well. But Maureen saw me looking and she closed the folder quickly, before I could read any more.

YOUNG WOMAN WITH UNICORN

'Be still, Signora.'

A flurry behind the easel.

'Please, Signora. Please.'

This studio's so hot, and these robes make it even worse. I shall die if I have to sit here for much longer.

At least the dog is finally asleep. I couldn't get it to stay still, squirming in my arms, and all the time the artist screeching with exasperation: 'Signora, please!' So fussy; they all are, though this one's not bad-looking. Younger than the others.

He keeps fiddling with the backdrop, repositioning it to catch the light. In the painting I will be sitting on a balcony, above a winding road, with blue hills stretching into the distance, though the hills look nothing like the hills back home in Canino; no farmhouses or tavernas, no lovingly-tended olive trees.

'Why do I need this stupid dog anyway?' I say, as he

flicks my hair over my shoulders once again.

'Because when I am finished, Signora,' he says proudly, 'the dog will have become a unicorn.'

A unicorn? Bet this was *his* idea.

The first time I saw him was two years ago, on the day Orsino and I were married. He looked magnificent, towering above us at the altar. Maybe it was the scent of flowers, or the sonorous plainchant in Latin, but when I looked up at him I felt dizzy. He was so sleek, so assured, his vestments shimmering as he intoned the blessing of the vows. A prince of the church; isn't that what they're called, cardinals? And all through the ceremony he was staring at me. I was so excited, and also a little bit afraid. Because even though I was getting married, I knew what was going to happen.

Orsino had never stared at me like that. Not much to look at, Orsino Orsini. A bit weedy. And that squint! 'One eye's so lovely, the other keeps looking at it,' my younger sister sniggered. 'Wait till you're sixteen, Isabella,' I said, 'and see who they find for you.' Orsino was eager and awkward and happy, just like any other seventeen year old, I suppose, but his mother Adrianna was happiest of all. You could almost see the light of the 3,000 gold florins my father had paid glinting in her eyes. She'd put the whole thing together: Orsino would have had no chance of marrying someone like me without his mother's scheming. '*Step*-mother,' Orsino corrected. At the banquet she drew me aside, her fingernails like talons digging into my arms as I was returning to the table. 'You are a lucky woman,' she said, inclining her dark head not at Orsino, but at *him*, sitting three seats down from Orsino, staring hungrily at me. 'Some day,' Adrianna said, 'some day, that man will be Pope.'

I walk each day from the palace to the studios in my new gemstone-encrusted sandals. Claudio accompanies me. He's pathetic, Claudio, with his limp and his withered claw of a left hand. He follows me everywhere. This isn't my idea, or Claudio's; *he* insisted. 'You must always be accompanied,' he'd said, 'for your safety. I don't wish to lose you.' He's never said he loves me, but I know he does. And although I shuddered when introduced to Claudio, I'm getting used to him, shuffling sadly a couple of steps behind me. He says very little, but he notices lots of things. Everywhere in this city you can smell the stinking murky river. As we cross over a bridge Claudio points downstream. At first I can't make out anything, but then I see; further down, at the water's edge, boatmen are hauling out the morning's grim catch. Four dead, it looks like. Crowds used to gather, craning to get a better view of the sodden corpses. But a body in the Tiber isn't big news these days.

These sittings are so boring; studio after studio, in these ridiculous gowns.

He keeps making me do it. Six months ago it was some saint, and six months before that it was the Virgin Mary. Me, the Virgin! 'Bit late for that,' I say to him in the bedchamber. He's still stretched out between the sheets, sucking on grapes. Very pleased with himself.

'But why not?' he says, reaching over to the fruit bowl and expertly twisting a few more off the stalk. 'You have all the essential qualities to be the Mother of Christ, my child.' He smirks at me then; he knows I hate it when he calls me 'child'.

'No doubt my reward will be in Heaven,' I say, sitting back down on the bed. 'But something in the meantime would be nice.'

'We'll see,' he says, an eyebrow lifting as he pulls me towards the pillows.

Within a year of the wedding, everything had been arranged. Adrianna again: my move to Rome, the new 'position' in the palace, everything. 'What a wonderful opportunity,' she said, catching my eye when Orsino wasn't looking. Not too bright, Orsino. He visits me once a month; Adrianna makes sure all niceties are observed. Even Claudio stares at him curiously. Poor Orsino. He is kind and attentive, always telling me how much he loves me. But surely he can see what's happening here?

The maids bring me my clothes. Today I select a silver-hemmed tunic. So much to choose from: silk, and cotton, and *reticella* lace, all so beautiful. And this afternoon my brother Guido calls on me, again. He's so needy, Guido; at times he infuriates me, pacing up and down the room fretting about whether I've asked yet, and when will I know. 'It is not I who wants this, Giulia,' he says then, pompously. 'It is God who calls me to wear the red hat of the cardinal.' 'Guido,' I say, 'I'll do what I can. But stop this nonsense about God.' He looks sheepish for a moment, but decides not to argue; I'm his best chance, and he knows it.

Although he's Pope, he's not even Italian. The family are originally from Spain, apparently. Lucia explained it all. She also lives in the palace. A little older than me; she is very nearly beautiful. Is she his sister or his daughter? Occasionally we walk together in the palace gardens, her and me, flirting with the gardeners. In the end-wall beside the flower-beds there is a door, leading (this is supposed to be a secret) through an alley to his residence. He rarely comes by day, except sometimes to visit Lucia. (She *is* his daughter, the more I think of it, although she never says). At night I can hear the little garden door squeak open, the footsteps hurrying towards me, up the path. 'How can you not hear that door?' I ask him one night. 'Maybe love is deaf as well as blind?' I say. He laughs, says nothing. But the next day two groundsmen come to the garden to replace the hinges.

The puppy is awake, yelping and wriggling.

'It's too hot in here, I told you,' I say. But that's not why he woke; the little runt must have felt it also, the movement inside me. A kick, and then another. 'Like a butterfly fluttering in your stomach,' the nurse says when eventually I ask that she come to see me. Dry old bitch, that one; how would she know? 'Signor Orsini will be so pleased,' I smile back. 'Pah!' she says, as she hobbles out of the bed-chamber and down the corridor.

Later that evening when *he* calls I say nothing. He's worried; there's going to be a war soon. France again. He needs to raise an army. And there's the new St Peter's to be built, the old cathedral crumbling, ready to fall down. 'Where am I supposed to find the money for all this?' he groans, slumping on the bed. Then he looks at me and smiles, and produces from the folds of his robe a gift; a box containing a ruby the size of a clementine, on a golden chain. We lie together, and later he gestures towards the tapestry from the House of Este on the wall opposite the bed. 'The symbol of the penetration of the human by the Divine,' he says, pointing at the unicorn, 'untameable by anyone — except a virgin.' He starts talking about allegory and incarnation, though I can't follow what he's saying. But the ruby's nice. I ask him to help me put it on. 'You won't forget Guido,' I say, as he fastens the hasp. The chain feels a little tight around my neck.

The next night, though, I can't keep it a secret any longer. So I tell him.

He *seems* pleased. 'This is…wondrous news,' he says quietly. Then he looks out the window. 'The gift of issue for the Orsini family. Let us pray for both of you it will be a son.'

In the bed sheets I turn towards him. 'You know

Orsino had nothing to do with this.'

He glances at me quickly, a little flash of anger in his eyes, then looks away again. 'I did not say he did, my child. But you have had congress recently with him, have you not?'

It's true, but... 'That's not what happened.' My voice catches as I speak. 'This is yours,' I say. 'Your child. *Ours*.'

'Hush now,' he says, stretching his arm across my shoulders. But he's still looking out the window, and he doesn't draw me to him.

Guido calls a few days later; he is to get his red hat after all. 'This is God's will, Giulia,' he says earnestly, promising to say a thousand Masses for me. 'Cardinale delle gonne,' one of the younger maids — a new cheeky one — whispers as he leaves. *The cardinal of the skirts.* She looks worried when she realises I have heard, but I just smile weakly. All I can think of is my baby. Everyone in the palace seems to know. I even saw Claudio glancing at my belly the other day, when he thought I wasn't looking. 'Yes Claudio,' I say, 'it's true; aren't you pleased for me?' He starts to say something but then he stops, and looks away.

Is this picture ever going to be finished? At least I no longer have to hold that stupid dog. But now even sitting in the one spot for any length of time is difficult. 'Are you sure you are comfortable, Signora?' says the artist — Raphael, his name is — as he smoothes the folds of my skirt. Quite attractive, this Raphael, if a bit girlish. I wonder does he prefer men? He never looks at me the way other men do. Or did; I'm a good few months gone now, swollen like a goose being fattened for Christmas. 'Cheer up, Claudio,' I say as we cross the bridge, heading back; I'm wearing one of those soft billowy smocks. Claudio shakes his head dolefully; there's something worrying him, I know, but he won't tell me. The heat in the city these days is almost unbearable. Even at night the air is stifling; there's no escape. I want to sleep and yet I can't; and when I do, I keep having this dream, again and again. I am standing alone at the edge of a midnight forest. And then I hear the sound of someone — something — approaching, leaves and branches being brushed aside as it lumbers towards me. Suddenly it crashes out into the clearing, panting, steam rising from its flanks, the moonlight silvering its terrible horned head.

The new maid opens the door of the bedchamber to allow him in. I can hear her giggling; he says something to her, but I can't make out what it is. Sofia, her name is. She's here more and more, floating around in her white muslin dress. I thought I saw her in the gardens yesterday walking with Lucia and him. I tried to catch Lucia's eye, but she just looked away. When he visits, he's distracted; we try to have congress, but it's too uncomfortable for me to lie underneath. 'Very well,' he says, turning over with a sigh.

I try to talk to him. 'Who will you have paint me next?' I ask. 'Pintoricchio, perhaps?' Old goat, Pintoricchio; hands everywhere.

He grunts non-committally.

'Maybe a picture of the Presentation of the Infant Jesus?' I say.

'Maybe,' he says, biting on a plum.

I try again. 'I hear the new maid, Signorina Berghenti, is most obliging,' I say.

'Sofia?' he says. Ah; he's interested now alright.

'Yes,' I say. 'I hear she has obliged the head-gardener, and one of the sentries, and the day-cook also. How unfortunate one so obliging should also have the pox.'

He pauses for a moment, the plum halfway to his lips.

'Far more grievous than the sin of lust is the sin of envy,' he says, eyeing me steadily, before he resumes. His teeth tear into the silky darkness of the fruit's flesh, and for a moment he does not speak.

'When I was a law student in Bologna,' he says eventually, 'our elderly tutor gave us a piece of advice.' He's chomping noisily as he talks, his mouth full. '"For a happy union", the tutor told us, "the wife must be blind, and the husband deaf."' He spits out the plum-stone and looks at me again. 'Was he right, do you think?'

I don't say anything. A rivulet of juice trickles down his chin.

This painting is almost done. At the end of the final sitting I ask to see it, but Raphael demurs. 'It is better if you wait, Signora, until it is finished.' But I insist, and he relents. Not bad, I suppose, but is my forehead quite so high? My waist looks so small; much smaller than it is now. And the little runty dog has grown — as promised — a horn out of the top of his head.

Afterwards I waddle back towards the palace. Claudio has to stop every so often to let me catch my breath. My belly feels enormous; the time must be near. We move slowly through the crowds, the stalls where bellowing traders hawk their wares, and we are almost at the palace when Claudio puts his good hand on my arm and steers me into a little chapel. 'Why are we praying, Claudio?' I say as he nudges me up the side aisle and stops at one of the pews. The chapel is almost empty. It's a relief to be in out of the sun, and I sit down. Claudio looks at me, his eyes glittering; are they tears? 'What's wrong, Claudio?' I say, but he just shakes his head, pointing to a painting on the wall: a woman trying to protect her baby from a soldier, the soldier slashing her with his sword as he rips the baby from her arms. Her shawl and shirt are soaked in blood; the baby, open-mouthed, is screaming. I look again at Claudio; his withered hand gesturing repeatedly at the picture as his breath comes quicker and quicker. 'What *is* it, Claudio?' I ask again, and he is just about to speak when a priest emerges from a side-door near the altar, glances over at us and then glides down the centre aisle. 'Nothing,' Claudio mutters, looking over not at me but at the priest. Then he looks behind him, and surveys carefully the length and breadth of the chapel. 'Come on,' he says, motioning towards the door we came in. 'We should leave.'

In the bedchamber the maids fuss and cluck, arranging jugs and towels. The nightshirt I have on is one the nurse gave me: it's frayed and worn.

There is no sign of *him*; but then, there hasn't been any sign for days, of anyone. Not even Claudio; when I ask about him, one of the older maids shakes her head quickly. I know there's a rumour that another corpse was pulled from the river two days ago, a corpse with a claw for a left hand.

'Your time has come,' the nurse says, leaning behind me to plump up a pillow. 'Whatever is God's will, will be,' she says then, looking at me pityingly.

The ruby catches her eye. 'Oh no,' she says, 'we can't allow this.'

She motions to the maids for assistance; one steps forward. Sofia.

'Too dangerous,' the old hag continues as Sofia unclasps the chain. 'You might choke during the delivery. Signorina Berghenti will keep it safe until we are finished.' I lie back on the bed and wait for what comes next, the kicks inside me getting stronger, like hooves approaching from a distance.

AWAY GAME

The fitting was one of those shower/bath affairs. He'd pulled the plunger up to the 'shower' setting, but it kept slipping back. He tried to jam it in position with one of the little bottles of shampoo the hotel provided; the water briefly sprinkled his hair before cascading once more over his feet. He jerked the plunger up again and held it there; he almost had to crouch to keep it in place. This wasn't going to work, he thought. Maybe he should have a bath instead.

He put the plug in and let the plunger down, and as he did he heard her call his name. The bath was filling quickly. He reached down to swirl the water; it was silky, warm. When had he last had a *bath*? He couldn't actually remember. As he lowered himself she called his name again, more urgent this time.

'Paul!'

He leaned back against the enamel. The bath's dimensions did not allow him to stretch out full-length. Over the sound of the flowing water he could hear the TV in the bedroom being turned up loud.

'I'm in the bath!' he said.

'You might want to see this,' she replied.

He sighed and turned off the taps. Hauling himself out of the tub, he reached for one of the bathrobes, pausing to consider his reflection before opening the door.

The TV was blaring; the sound of it filled the room. Maggie was sitting on the bed, the Room Service menu she'd been flicking through open beside her.

'This is awful,' she said. 'So awful.'

He stared at the TV. The man with the microphone had his back to the terminal. A ribbon of red text ran along the bottom of the screen: *Irish Plane Crash-Lands in Heathrow.* Paul could hear the whine of sirens as emergency vehicles streamed away. The reporter was struggling to make himself heard. 'Flight EI 166 was filled with Irish fans,' he said, 'all travelling for this evening's play-off. But in light of this,' — and here he turned to gesture towards the runway — 'already it's being suggested that the game should not be played.'

The remote: where was the remote? He scanned the room; the crumpled bed sheets, the tiny bedside lockers, the dresser where Maggie had laid out her make-up, hair-brush, perfume.

'Can we turn this *down*?' he said.

'Ok, ok,' said Maggie. She began rummaging between the sheets. The remote was under the Room Service menu. 'Here,' she said, pushing the control over to the side where earlier he'd lain. She looked up at him then, and patted the empty space beside her.

He muted the sound. The screen was showing a diagram of the aircraft, with a circle around the wheels of the landing-gear, and an arrow towards the fuel lines. *Equipment failure,* said the tickertape below. It was definitely the same flight. He'd printed out the details, sticking them underneath a fridge-magnet in the kitchen so Jane could see them. In the hallway of their home, when he'd kissed Jane and the two boys goodbye, and told them that he'd see them all tomorrow, he'd been wearing the green-and-white supporters' scarf, the scarf now stuffed inside the coat he'd thrown on the chair in this room when they'd arrived.

Maggie shifted slightly to her right. 'You wanna sit down?' she said.

He squeezed past the dressing table and perched on the edge of the opposite side of the bed, facing away from her. The remote was still in his hand. He dabbed the volume button once, twice, and the sound came back, the voices in the studio now a murmur. Kelly, he thought, and Ryan. And Clarkey too, Clarkey went to all the games.

'I know them,' he said.

Maggie turned towards him. 'Know who?'

'The plane,' he said. He kept looking at the screen. 'A few from work. We'd said we'd go.'

He hadn't actually explained to them why he'd pulled out. 'Something's come up,' he'd said, and when Ryan asked was it to do with home he'd said, 'Yeah, that kind of thing.' They'd nodded then, and let the matter drop, though later Clarkey'd asked him if everything was alright. 'Fine, fine,' he'd said, and Clarkey'd slapped him on the back and said sure they'd all be going to the Finals when Ireland won, and that already he'd been checking out the prices. 'Yeah, definitely,' Paul had said, 'put me down for that, for sure.'

An aeronautical engineer was onscreen, talking about struts and rivets, and how much fuel a jet this size would carry as the newsreader listened gravely. The wardrobe beside the TV was slightly open. Paul could see inside a sliver of the green silk dress Maggie'd brought to wear to dinner later, the dress he'd so admired when he'd first met her. It hung there in the wooden darkness, an emerald ghost. This had been her idea: a night together in this city. 'Paris,' she'd whispered, after they'd done it for the first time, in his car, 'wouldn't it be great if we could go to Paris?'

He tossed the remote back onto the bed and tightened the cord on his bathrobe. He was aware of her beside him; she'd scooched across the bed to where he was sitting.

'That's terrible,' she said, and she put her arm around him. He could smell the drink off her breath. 'Oh Paul,' she said, nuzzling his cheek, 'I'm so sorry.'

Her arm felt meaty on his shoulders. Was she drunk, he wondered. She couldn't be; they'd only ordered the one bottle, and they hadn't even finished it.

She leaned in. The heat of her, the weight, surprised him.

'We need some air in here,' he said, shrugging her arm

away. He stood up. The room was not much wider than the bed; in three strides he was at the window. He turned the handle and tried to push the window outwards, but it would only open a few inches. He pulled it shut and yanked at it again, harder this time, but still it would not budge. 'Just... leave it, Paul,' Maggie said. He tried it again, managing this time to prise the window open a little further. The street was narrow, quiet, a side-street really, though he could hear not far away the sounds of cars and horns. He pressed his face into the gap and tried to breathe deeply.

'Do I know any of them?' she said.

He half-turned back into the room. She had the sheets pulled up around her, almost to her chin. 'Paul?'

Why was she asking him these questions?

'You might have... met them once,' he said.

She had, actually. 'This is Maggie,' he'd said over the laughter and the chink of glasses in their Friday evening haunt. 'She works with me.' Kelly'd just stared at him. Ryan had started making those big *oh-ho* eyes, and then Clarkey smirked and put his arm around her. 'God break your cross, love,' he'd said, flirting with her the way he did with every woman he met, even though he'd never go offside, never. But so what if she'd met them; what did it matter? He turned away again. Across the street a shop was selling cheap T-shirts piled in mounds in the front window, and on the corner there was a graffiti-covered wooden door, with an outside table and two chairs beneath a sign saying *Café-Bar-Tabac*.

'Oh, *those* guys,' said Maggie. He heard her lift the wine glass, take a sip. 'They were *cool*.'

Christ, she was drunk. He spread his hands out either side of the sill.

'There was a big guy, Clarke…'

'…Clarkey. George Clarke,' he said. He could not look at her.

'Clarkey, yeah!' she said. 'Oh, he was lovely.'

Paul spun around. What entitlement had she to talk about these men? They were *his* friends, not hers; and now, unless they'd been very lucky, they were probably…

His mobile phone was in his coat-pocket. He reached over to fish it out and powered it on. *You have 4 missed calls.* The phone bleeped twice then, an accusation. *You have 2 new text messages. We love you so much.* Jane's mobile. *Please please be OK. XXX.* The two boys would be sitting at the kitchen-table, still in their football gear, squabbling over sausages as the Saturday Sport radio programme murmured in the background. He imagined his wife suddenly telling them to be *quiet please, QUIET, for heaven's sake* as the news from Heathrow started coming in, biting her lip as she checked the print-out on the fridge.

He put the phone down. There was a champagne glass on the bedside locker, half-full, although the bubbles had disappeared. He raised the glass briefly to his lips. It tasted sweet, and flat.

'Those poor guys,' Maggie was saying. She had her hands clasped round her knees which she'd drawn up to her chest. The bed creaked as she rocked back and forth. 'Those poor, poor guys.' The way she dragged out the word 'guys,' in that mid-Atlantic drawl of hers, which made no sense, since she was not American, she'd never even been to America, so far as he knew. 'I mean, to think that they're just *gone*,' she said, and as she spoke she began to weep.

He stood looking at her, his hands on his hips. His bathrobe had started working itself loose again; he yanked it tight.

'I don't believe this,' he said.

'I know,' said Maggie. She clutched the bed sheet, a small white bunch in her fist. 'Isn't it just so...'

'...Can we just stop talking, please?' he said. He felt it rising inside him, a rolling wave of rage, and he couldn't stop it, he didn't want to stop it.

'What do you mean?' said Maggie. Her smudged mascara made her look like she'd been punched in both eyes, hard. 'Paul?'

'Just...never mind,' he said. On the TV a woman was speaking in an almost whisper about death and families; he could barely hear her. *Bereavement Counsellor*, the caption said.

'Jesus, Paul,' said Maggie. She heaved herself up off the bed and waddled across the room. At the bathroom door she stopped, her hand on the handle, and looked back at him. 'You're such a...such a...'

He slumped back on the bed as the bathroom door slammed. Briefly he closed his eyes; when he opened them the light in the street had faded further, the room now almost in gloom. He reached over to flick one of the switches: the bed, the chair, the room were all suddenly soaked in the overhead lamp's yellow glare. He squatted at the mini-bar, which was empty. From inside the bathroom he could hear water running as well as the sound of angry breathless sobs. He dressed quickly. 'Back soon,' he muttered towards the bathroom as he left. In the hotel lobby a TV was showing the press conference: the two football associations were postponing the match as a mark of respect for the dead. The receptionist grimaced perfunctorily at him as he went through the entrance and out onto the street. The pavements were empty. He turned left and crossed over, heading for the tabac.

At the counter the Algerian assistant motioned to the seats outside when Paul asked for a *café au lait*. He sat in one of the spindly metal chairs. It was colder than he had expected. The Algerian brought the coffee and the bill: €3.50. Paul handed him a €5 and waved away the change. The Algerian nodded and disappeared. Paul placed his mobile on the table and poured sugar from the sachet into the cup. Her fault; this was all Maggie's fault. Any moment now she'd call him, but he would not answer. She'd leave a message, demanding to know where he was and what did he think he was doing, walking out of the hotel room and leaving her like that. Later, much later, he would explain. The shock, he'd say. He'd mention his dead companions, recite their names. He'd tell her how he'd needed space; still did, in fact. He'd come up with something. A goal in the last minute; *something.* He sipped his coffee; already it had cooled. A street lamp brightened beside him, then another, and another. His phone began to pulse, vibrating on the table as it sang out its tinny tune. He leaned forward to see the caller's name flashing on the screen. *Home,* it blinked, again and again. *Home. Home. Home.*

OSTRICH

By then there were nine of us left in the minibus. The others had got out at Portbane, with shouts of 'See you tomorrow', and slaps on the side and the back doors. If we'd looked we could have seen them through the back window; we could have watched them walking away into the night, Sammy and Davy and Tommy and Harry T, the glow of Harry T's cigarette rising and falling as he limped alongside the others into the darkness. We could have said goodbye. But we didn't; we sat back, spreading ourselves into the spaces left and continuing the banter we'd been at all the way home from Bests, and we were still at it as we came to the top of the hill when Stuey let one go. It was definitely Stuey; a small self-satisfied trumpet blast, the stink quickly filling the air. 'Jesus, Stuey,' said Steven, waving his hands theatrically to get rid of the smell. Others joined in, Billy and Gerald and Gordon and Harry O, all groaning and fanning the air. 'Open a window, Dickie,' said Johnnie. He'd worked longer in Bests than any of us, Johnnie, he was just about to retire. 'For Chrissakes, open a window.' Stuey just kept laughing and saying it wasn't him, though he knew we knew it was. Dickie wound the driver's window down halfway, and as the January night air rushed in we all leaned forward, even Stuey, inhaling with exaggerated relief, and it was then we saw at the bottom of the hill the light in the middle of the road.

Stella says I never talk about it. But I do, I do talk about it; I just don't always want to talk about it when she wants to talk about it. Anyway, what's to talk about? He's gone. Talking won't bring him back.

The light swung back and forth as the minibus came closer; it was a torch, signalling us to slow down. There were no other lights around; the road was dark and very quiet. 'What's he doing out here at this hour?' said Dickie, half to himself as he crunched down through the gears and prepared to stop. 'Police,' said Harry O. But as we neared we could see it wasn't the police; it was a man dressed in black, with some kind of hood covering his face, except for two big holes cut out for the eyes. 'Drive on, drive on,' shouted Johnnie. But the minibus had almost stopped, its headlights lighting up the road and hedges like a stage, and under the beam of the lights the hedges seemed to dissolve as figures emerged onto the road, in front of us and beside us and behind us. Dickie was trying to get the minibus into gear again, to get it going, but already there was someone at the driver's door, trying to yank it open. There were others on the passenger side and at the back doors as well, banging and shouting. Harry O tried to hold the handles shut but the back doors were flung open and there were four of them outside, pointing what looked like guns and screaming 'Get out, the lot of youse, get out.'

We'd bought a pram, a cot; lots of things, so that we'd be ready. We were so young ourselves; I mean, this was nearly fifteen years ago. He lived for four days. The doctor knew as soon as he was born that he wasn't going to make it. I saw him in the incubator. I don't know about these things, but he looked long, lying there; one of the nurses said he would have been tall, like me. I liked that. I never cried, though Stella couldn't stop crying. The hospital allowed her to stay in an extra night. On her last day before she came home I was sitting beside the bed while she was asleep, just looking at her, when the consultant came in. The tie he was wearing had lots of golf-balls on it. 'This one just wasn't meant to be,' he said. I couldn't think how to reply, so I just said 'Ach, sure, I know, doctor.' He looked at the chart at the end of the bed, and then at Stella; she was still asleep. 'Ye were lucky to have gotten as far as ye did,' he said. He shook my hand, and said goodbye, and then he left. I think I knew what he meant; Stella'd been four weeks short of full term when it happened. But it didn't feel like we'd been lucky.

We clambered out into the night and they were shoving us between the minibus and the ditch until we got to the front. Johnnie and Dickie were already there, two men either side of them. The engine was switched off but the minibus's headlights were still on, making Johnnie and Dickie look very pale; and I thought, Jesus, if someone doesn't start the engine the lights'll soon drain the battery right down, and then one of them (the Hood, I think) said 'Right, which of youse is a Pape?'

One of the other doctors, a younger one, did say it would be good if we could talk about it. But who would you talk to? Not the boys in Bests. There was enough going on in Bests anyhow. Morgan, the foreman, was a right bastard to our lot, though there were less and less of our crowd working there; just me, and O'Neill up in Orders, and McCollum in the wages office. But you wouldn't be talking to them, nor to the other lot either. The younger ones, Gordon and Harry O, would be sniggering as Morgan stomped red-faced up and down the factory floor bellowing about production numbers and how he could find plenty to replace us. 'He just doesn't like you, Ollie,' Gerald said in the canteen, looking at me with those big sad bloodhound eyes. 'You could come in here on a white horse wearing a Rangers jersey and an Orange sash shouting 'Up King Billy' and 'Fuck the Pope', and Morgan still wouldn't like you. It's nothing got to do with you not being a Prod.' I like Gerald. But I didn't talk to him about it neither.

Gordon and Harry O were shaking their heads as we all stood on the side of the road. One of them, a boy no more than sixteen, though big enough all the same, walked up and down the line, stopping to shine a torch in each of our faces. Gerald was second last; I was last. As the torch came closer Gerald tugged my sleeve, once, quickly. 'Say nothing, say nothing,' he said. The boy came to Gerald and gave him a little shove as he jiggled the beam in his face. And then he came to me.

Back when it happened, there were lots of people calling to the door. Eileen Leahy carried round a big pot of stew, and the Donohoe girls brought plates of sandwiches and cakes, but no one mentioned it. Father McElhone said how sorry he was, and on the altar he'd gone on about God's will. But no one ever once asked 'So Ollie, how does it feel to have lost your baby, your son?' Only baby, as it happened. I think everyone was just afraid to talk about it. In McGeeney's shop there were shy nods from other customers, and old McGeeney came out from the store-room to shake my hand and say it was 'a bad business'. The day after the funeral I went down to the Dew Drop Inn on my own, just to get out of the house. It was late afternoon and there was no one in the place except for Traps McFadden, sitting on his usual stool at the far end of the bar. Traps bred greyhounds and was a bit touched. I'd never spoken to him, but as soon as I came in he saluted me, and beckoned me over. 'Sorry for your trouble,' he said hoarsely. 'But they're good stock, the O'Tierneys,' he continued. Stella's family. 'Sure, she'll whelp again.' 'Hush now, Traps,' said Brendan behind the bar, setting down a glass in front of him, 'don't be bothering the poor man.' I sat down at one of the tables. Brendan brought me over a whiskey but refused to accept any money, and went back to sit on a stool behind the counter, drinking a mineral. Nobody said anything. Sure what was the point? Talking wasn't going to solve anything.

I could smell the beer off him. But there was something else, another smell; the smell of chips. Nights outside the takeaway when I first started out with Stella; the two of us with a skinful on board, each holding a warm bag, the vinegar slathered on and already beginning to stain the bag in patches, and the salt glistening like little snowflakes on the golden chunks as we ate them, Stella and me. Sometime this evening, before he'd hidden in the hedges on the side of this road, waiting, this boy had got his hands on some beer, and then he'd had chips. The torch he was carrying wasn't really a torch; it was a bicycle lamp and he was shining it in my eyes. He turned to the Hood, the light still jiggling in my face. 'This one here,' he said, his voice rising in excitement. 'The big lanky fella. This here's one.'

The last time it had been mentioned, we were on the couch, watching telly. The news was showing a funeral: more than one, actually; there were three of them. They were being carried in to the graveyard, coffin after coffin, like they were coming off an assembly line. 'Why do you never go?'

she asked. 'Go where?' I said. 'You know where,' she said. 'The grave. James's grave.' James had been Stella's father's name as well. The cameras were showing the crowds gathering around the opened ground, crying and sighing and dabbing at their eyes. 'Ach, don't start this again,' I said. 'But you don't,' she said. 'Like an ostrich, so you are, Ollie, with your head stuck in the sand.' She was almost shouting now. 'A big ostrich, that's what you are.' I didn't say anything. On the telly a priest was saying some prayers, and then it was back to the newsreader, talking in front of a picture of a building that had been blown apart earlier that day. After a minute or two Stella got up from the couch. I could hear her clattering around with the kettle and the teapot in the kitchen, and I knew she was crying.

How did this boy know me, know who I was? There must have been a moment when he'd seen me. In McGeeney's, perhaps. Or the Dew Drop Inn, he could have been there one evening when I'd been there. Maybe he'd been waiting anxiously at the counter, hoping to be served. But how did he know? Unless he'd seen me outside St Mary's, in the car-park, after Mass. I couldn't remember ever having seen him before, anywhere. Maybe he worked in Bests once, though I didn't think so. But he knew me somehow, knew me well enough to know. The Hood came over, and there was shouting as he grabbed me and dragged me back down behind the minibus. Gerald's voice: 'Leave him be,' he was saying. Dickie was shouting too; 'It's alright, he's one of us!' Gordon and Harry O said nothing. 'Right,' said the Hood.

He adjusted something on his gun; there was a little click. He stepped slightly away from me, as if to get a better angle. There were still two of them standing either side of me, but when he motioned to them they stood apart. 'Right,' he said again. 'Now get you down that road, and don't look back.'

She's wrong. I did go once, about two months after he died. Outside the gate a man was selling flowers, and just inside the entrance there was a woman in a little hut who asked my name and directed me, though it still took me a while to find the grave again. There were flowers there from the last time Stella'd been, laid carefully at the foot of the little headstone that gave his name and the date when he was born, and the other date, four days later. And underneath, the words *With The Angels Once More*, which Stella had wanted. I knelt down and started to say a little prayer, and then I stopped. None of this prayer stuff would make any sense to him. So instead I just said his name. 'Well, James,' I said, 'you poor wee fella.' I could feel my eyes starting to well up. 'You poor wee mite,' I said. Then I quickly wiped away the tears and coughed; a woman a few rows down glanced over at me. I stood up and headed for the entrance. And I never told Stella. I don't know why I didn't tell her, but I didn't.

I started running away into the darkness. I could hear gunfire. Any moment now, I thought, one of these will hit me. The shots kept coming, little muted whip-cracks. But there was another sound, over the sound of gunshots and the sound of my shoes slapping the tarmac; it was the sound of men screaming, crying out in pain. I kept running, though: I didn't dare turn round to see what was happening in the dip of the road that was still lit up by the headlights of the minibus. I kept running on my big long ostrich legs, and I never looked back.

PARTNERS

In the darkened hallway Roland could smell the roses. The firm had sent them, last Monday; a little personal touch they prided themselves on, sending bouquets to the wives of the partners who'd been forced to work the whole weekend in the office, again. They lay on the hall table, still in their cellophane, along with the accompanying card. *To Nikki, compliments of Sweeney Fletcher Anderson & Co.* She'd torn the card in two. It's their way of saying sorry, he'd tried to explain the first time they'd sent them; that, and the bonus. Especially the bonus. 'A couple of years, that's all.' Already Roland was the youngest partner ever; if he kept going, soon he'd be Managing Partner, and then… 'Just, no more roses, ok?' Nikki'd said. 'Of course,' he'd soothed. But still the flowers arrived.

He headed out the front door and sat into the car. As he gunned the engine he felt a small dart of pain in his foot. Really, he thought, this business with the flowers was her problem, not his. All those tears and broken crockery were because *her* career had...well, stalled. 'Resting,' wasn't that what actors called it when they couldn't get any work? Maybe this new play would make something happen; and then again, maybe it wouldn't. €urobola was about a deadly virus spread by handling money. 'It's a, a, a ...searing indictment of the world wuh, wuh, wuh...we live in,' Reggie had stammered over the white tablecloth in the restaurant where Nikki had dragged Roland along to meet the proud author-director. 'Do you think Sweet FA might wuh, wuh, wuh...want to sponsor?' *'Dweeb,'* Roland had wanted to scream but didn't as he looked across at Reggie's earnest face, his ridiculous sideburns, his cheap school-swot glasses. And those expensive shoes, poking out from under the table; what kind of anarchist wore Tuttys, anyway? 'Sweeney Fletcher Anderson,' he'd replied, ignoring Reggie's casual deployment of the firm's nickname, 'have always been committed to the arts.' Maybe the firm would throw a few quid in; he might even ask—after he'd seen off Cronin. Dympna Cronin was Roland's one remaining rival for Managing Partner; fair-haired, plump, old-school, first in the car park, last in the office. And no fool; she'd very nearly caught him out a couple of years back, when Roland's draft of a merger agreement failed to take account of a recent change in M & A legislation. Roland had managed to blame his trainee, a girl named Andrea Harper who was escorted red-eyed from the building, but it had been a narrow escape.

The city glittered in the violet pre-dawn. A red light

briefly halted his progress. He nodded amiably at the driver of the sleek new car beside him: white shirt, vivid tie, a dark suit jacket hung in the back. How prosperous this city had once again become, with more and more men like him — and even some women, he thought — rising and dressing in the dark, on the road before daybreak, determined to make their mark, to take what was rightfully theirs. After the bleakness of the last five years it was like landing on the shores of a new world, a world in which he and those like him were the new conquistadors, old-timers like Cronin left for dead. *Conquistador*: might be a good name for a yacht.

His car glided through the junction and up onto the bridge past the sleeping forms huddled under blankets against the railings. The great galleon of the building came into view. Around the shimmering lake waters of the entrance plaza artfully-placed bronze ducks maintained their Zen stillness. The firm's title hung above the main doorway, in letters of block gold; how might the names be reconfigured, he wondered, so as to accommodate his own? As he descended the ramp into the underground car park he noticed again the little stabbing pain, in both feet now; some sort of gout perhaps, or even something worse? He was young and fit, but maybe he should visit the firm's surgery for a check-up, just in case. Three of the partners had had heart attacks in the last eighteen months, including Quinn, Managing Partner, and now about to retire, whose job and corner-office would surely soon be his. And anyway, thought Roland, easing the car into its usual spot, he'd need to be in the whole of his health from here on in, now that he was going to be a father.

He undid his seat belt and sat for a moment smiling ruefully to himself. Nikki hadn't told him her secret, but he knew. They'd had the children/no children conversation two years ago, before they'd married, Nikki agreeing then that there was no room for a baby. But lately he'd known something was up; she really was a pretty hopeless actor. He'd found the box for the testing kit while putting out the bins two days ago. At first he'd been furious, although he'd managed to restrain himself from confronting her. At least this explained her unsettled mood, and her lack of enthusiasm between the sheets in recent weeks, which she'd claimed was down to the intensity of rehearsals with bloody Reggie. He had begun then to imagine how it might be: the swaddled bundle of life in the crook of his elbow, women simpering around him. Someone (a boy, Roland was certain) to... *do* things with. His own father had been remote, austere; but he, Roland, would be different; he and Nikki. Thank God she hadn't developed a sudden craving for toothpaste, or coal. Even this morning, as he'd dressed as usual in the dark, groping beneath the bed for his shoes, he'd almost leaned over to kiss her on the forehead, and whisper *I know.* But in the end he had decided not to.

He exited at the seventh floor and hurried down the hushed corridor. Outside it was still dark, but a seam of light was breaking over the river in the east. He loved the way the city came alive in the mornings, although the view was not as good from his office as from Quinn's. He pictured how his appointment would happen: the farewell party for

Quinn, the stirring applause as his name was announced, and the frozen silence which would greet Cronin's 'retirement on health grounds'. As he daydreamed, he became aware of how uncomfortable his feet were; maybe if he gave them room to breathe whatever swelling there was might go down. He perched on the swivel chair and lifted his left heel onto his right knee. Undoing the lace of the black brogue he noticed a small scratch on the leather that he'd never seen before. The shoe did not come away easily. He undid the other one: a scuff mark on the toe was definitely new. Again an extra effort was required to prise it off, although the pain disappeared almost immediately. Maybe it wasn't gout after all. He picked up the left shoe to examine it. The eyeholes, the thin laces, the elaborate stitch patterns, these were all familiar, but there was something not quite right. He peered inside; there on the underside of the tongue in gold lettering was the manufacturer's name, faded in parts, although the *T* and *ys* were still visible. The dark luxurious interior of the shoe made it difficult to see in further, where his size — 9 ½, always and forever — was also inscribed. He loosened the laces and lifted up the tongue.

A gust of rain rattled against the window, as if someone had thrown pebbles at the glass. The forecast had mentioned the possibility of showers. The early morning sun was beginning to leak onto the streets, and in the slanting rain the high glass and shining steel of the offices across the river were burnished in a melancholy copper light. Roland sank back in his chair, his mouth slightly open, his heartbeat racing, his face suddenly hot.

Something was wrong here, something was terribly wrong. He stared into the shoe once more, as if by staring hard he could will the number into being. Where in God's name was the ½, he asked himself: the glass ½ full, the second ½, the other ½ — ah yes, indeed, his 'other half' — and what the *fuck* was going on? Slowly he lifted the other shoe, widening the sides so as to inspect the ox-coloured cave of its interior. Again he saw gold letters, the *Tutt* still visible — and again he saw the single digit, the one dialled in emergencies, a holed comma, a balloon adrift trailing its string, the tiny foetal embryo that was the number 9. Now he held them up together, side by side, the shoes he'd dug out from under his own bed that morning. If not mine, he thought, then *whose*, although in truth he already knew. In disbelief he gazed into them, the 9s in either hand morphing into a pair of immaculately-trimmed sideburns on a stammering, bespectacled, would-be theatre impresario. In *his* bed. With *his* —

'Everything alright, Roland?' said Quinn, who'd exercised the Managing Partner's prerogative of entering without knocking. He looked disdainfully at Roland's stockinged feet. 'Boardroom in fifteen,' he continued, 'it'll be official then, but I can tell you now, of course. I'm sure you've guessed anyway. May I present our new Managing Partner!' Roland nodded glumly as Dympna Cronin appeared over Quinn's shoulder, smiling wanly. 'A great choice, no doubt you'll agree,' said Quinn. Cronin glanced demurely at the carpet. 'Anyway, I'll leave you two to it. See you in the boardroom.' Cronin remained just inside the door. 'Well...congratulations, Dympna,' said Roland, padding over to her and extending his hand. 'Thank you,' said Cronin. She turned a polished heel and was about to leave when she stopped. 'By the way,' she said, waving a piece of paper, 'we might have a word about this. That M & A thing a little while ago; I got a letter. From Ms Harper.' She tapped the piece of paper. 'Not great reading, to be honest. Maybe you should take time off while we see if we can sort this out. We'll get you lawyered up, of course.' Roland was aware of a small hole in the toe of his left sock. 'All the same,' said Cronin, shaking her head, 'I wouldn't like to be in your shoes.'

A GREAT BIG BIBLE WIND

'So this woman,' Art said.

We were outside; it was still bright.

Richard was sitting on the big seat, beside Kath. His knee was touching Kath's. I was sitting at the far end of the table from the barbecue.

'This woman,' Art said, 'she suddenly starts running up and down the beach, shouting. Really loud.' Art was still wearing his shorts, and an apron; the apron had a full-length cartoon of a hot girl's body.

We'd been at the beach earlier, Art and me, and then we'd come home. 'A barbecue,' Art had said, 'why don't we ask Richard and Kath over?' Now there were plates scattered across the table, full of ribs and bones and dark-brown, dark-red smears that looked like wounds.

'We didn't know what she was going on about at first,' Art said, looking at me. 'We thought it was a fight. Sounded like a fight, didn't it, Mags?' 'Yeah,' I said, looking at Kath. She was wearing this white linen sun-dress, and she was looking at Art. At first I'd thought the dress was a little short, but maybe it was alright. Beside Richard's beige slacks her knees looked really brown.

'But it wasn't. A fight, I mean.' Art was poking at something on the barbecue with a knife. His legs were red and blotchy at the back, burnt from the seaside. Already they looked sore.

'She was pointing out to sea. "My son", she yelled. "Please, help my son."' Art took a swig of his beer, draining the bottle. He looked at the cooler. There were still a couple of beers left. 'Where's the thingy?' he said. 'Here,' I said, sliding the bottle-opener down the table.

'My son the doctor,' Richard said.

'What?' said Art, reaching into the cooler for a bottle. It didn't make sense, what Richard had said; Richard's sons were twelve and eight.

'You know that joke,' Richard said. He looked at Kath, who smiled back. 'The Cork mother. She's on the beach watching her son swimming, and then her son gets into trouble. So she runs up and down the beach shouting, "Help, help, my son the doctor is drowning." You know. Cork, like'. Richard put his hand on Kath's knee.

Art was trying to fit the opener over the top of the bottle. He'd had a few; we all had. Eventually he got it right, the bottle-cap flipping off and spinning to the ground. 'Good one,' he said, grinning at his friend.

'My grandmother was from Cork,' Kath said. She looked at Art and then across at me.

'Really?' said Art. He took a swig from the new bottle

and then wrapped it with his hand against his shoulder. 'Whereabouts?'

'Sure you don't know Cork,' I said.

'Yes I do,' said Art, giving me a quick look before turning back to Kath. He was holding his beer between his finger and thumb now, swinging it like he was counting time.

'So what happened?' said Richard.

Art stopped. 'Ah look, it's just... it's just boring,' he said, and looked away.

I could hear voices in the garden next door, and sizzling. They were still cooking. The barbecue-trays we'd bought on the way home from the beach had long since burned out.

'Oh please, Art, go on,' Kath said, leaning forward and smiling. Art looked at her and glanced at me again. He took another swig and said nothing.

'Jesus, Art,' I said, 'not the sulking. Please. I can't bear it.'

Kath looked at me. Kath was Richard's new girlfriend. Art had met her before, but this was my first time. She was younger than Emily, I thought, but not that much younger.

'I couldn't see anything,' Art said. 'But she could see. Couldn't you, Mags?' He looked at me and smiled. 'Eyes like a hawk,' he said. 'He was a good bit out,' I said, as a peace offering to my husband, 'but I could see he was in trouble.'

We were married the same year, Richard and Emily, and

Art and me. Richard and Art went way back; they'd graduated together, and worked in the same law firm, Freeman Waters. Before Emily'd had Pete and Gordy, and I'd had Ray, we'd gone on holidays together; Paris, and Nice, and Cannes. Richard liked France.

'Yeah, big trouble. He was drowning. Cork or not, Richard, huh?' Art was smiling at him. 'So she's losing it on the beach—and there's this guy, a surfer dude, a little way out, sitting on his board, waiting for the waves.'

'Cool,' said Kath. Tall, long fair hair. Richard had met her just over a year ago, a few months before he'd left Emily.

'This guy, anyway, this surfer dude, turns his board around and paddles out to the boy. And this boy was going down.'

'Not waving but drowning,' said Kath, taking a sip from her beer.

'How'd he get so far out?' Richard asked. He took a cigarette from the pack in front of him and put it to his lips. When he flicked the lighter a small flame came to life.

'Current,' Art said. 'The current's vicious.' He took another slurp. 'So he gets out to where the kid is. And he hauls him up! On to the board! Amazing. He starts paddling in, with the kid hanging on to the board. Everyone on the beach was watching; some people were even clapping. The boy's mother ran into the shallows to meet them. And she was crying now, she was pretty upset.'

'Who wouldn't be?' I said. I reached over for the wine

and poured out a three-quarter glass.

'Yeah, sure,' said Kath, nodding at me. She wasn't pretty, not really. But sexy, yes; she was sexy.

'She did thank him, I'm not saying she didn't.' Art was trying to be fair. 'The surfer dude, I mean. And the boy was upset too. I mean, he'd nearly drowned. He let go of the board in the shallows and kind of fell into her arms. And she was thanking the surfer guy and holding on to her son, really tight. And then, she started laying into him. Her kid. You know, slapping him and stuff. Slapping him on the head, full on.'

'Jesus,' said Richard. He took a drag of his cigarette.

'I know,' said Art. He moved over to the other chair and sat down. 'I mean, what's that about?'

'She only did it a few times, Art,' I said, taking a drink. 'She was *upset*, for God's sake.'

'I know all that, I know.' Art put his beer on the table. 'But how could she, how could she even think of doing something like that?'

'I'm not even sure it's legal,' said Richard. 'I think the government passed a law, a few years ago. Not to slap your child.'

I topped up my glass and took another drink, though I couldn't really taste anything. 'Art,' I said, waggling the almost empty bottle, 'do you think you could...?'

'Yeah, sure,' said Art. He didn't get up, though; instead, he reached over towards the cooler. 'Do you want a beer?' he said, dipping his hand into the ice that by now was mostly water.

'*No*, Art,' I said. 'Wine. I want a *wine*.' I waggled the

bottle again.

'Okay, okay,' Art said, getting to his feet. 'Anyone want anything else?' he said.

'No, I'm fine,' said Richard. 'I'm good,' said Kath, smiling.

'Back of the cupboard beside the fridge,' I called out as Art opened the kitchen door and went inside.

I took another drink and looked at Richard. His hair was silvery with little curls at the back, coiling over his collar. He looked like one of those early Roman emperors who was used to getting what he wanted.

Art returned with a six pack of beer and a bottle of white. He put the beers in the cooler and tore the foil off the top of the wine-bottle with the corkscrew. 'I mean, what gives her the right?' he said.

The last night in Cannes, our taxi was pulling up outside the restaurant when I realised I'd left my phone in the hotel. 'You don't need it,' Art said. But my father, Ray senior, had been ill, and I was worried the nursing-home might need to contact me. 'You guys order,' I said, 'I'll get this taxi back and join you in twenty minutes.' 'I'll come with you,' Richard had said then, 'I left mine behind as well.'

Art was twisting the corkscrew into the new bottle.

'Gives who the right?' said Richard, looking at Art.

'The woman,' Art said. 'The woman and her son.'

'Oh,' said Richard, pausing in the act of lifting his beer. 'We're still talking about *her*?'

'Well...yes,' said Art, pulling the cork out.

I pushed my empty glass towards him. He was always doing this, Art, going over and over the same thing; it was one of the reasons I'd stopped attending Group, though the other parents didn't seem to mind.

'I think,' Kath said, slowly, 'I think what she did was her way of showing her love.' She nodded to herself as she said this.

Art filled my glass, almost to the top. 'What do you mean?' he said.

I was looking at her as well.

'I mean,' Kath said, stroking the neck of the beer bottle with her finger, 'I mean, we all love each other in different ways, right?'

'Right,' said Art, though he didn't sound so sure.

'The way you love Mags,' Kath said, nodding at me, 'is different to the way I love Richard, or the way my father loves my mother, or the way Richard loves his sons.'

'Pete and Gordy,' I said.

Richard looked at me when I said their names, but didn't say anything.

'Pete and Gordy,' Kath said.

'And Ray,' said Art. 'The way we loved Ray, Mags and I.' He tried to catch my eye, but I wouldn't look at him.

'Ray as well,' Kath said, quietly. 'And what I'm saying is, we can't always explain how much we love them to the ones we love.'

'I still don't see,' Art was saying, 'what gives her the right to beat the shit out of her kid?'

'A few slaps, is all,' I said. 'Not "beat the shit". Come

on, Art.'

'It was more than a few slaps,' Art muttered.

The sun had now slipped down, and the garden next door was quiet.

'Look, Art,' Kath said, her big green eyes wide open. 'I'm not saying she was right. Of course I'm not suggesting you can beat up a child, for Christ's sake. What I mean is, this boy; she almost lost him. Almost. And so, getting him back like that, well, she wasn't just relieved, I'd say, but something more.'

Art was staring in Kath's direction, but I could tell he wasn't listening, not really. His eyes were glazed, and not just on account of the beer. He wasn't looking at her; he was looking past her. I knew that look, knew what it meant. He was thinking about Ray.

We'd been in the taxi rolling down the Croisette, that big road lined with palm trees when I'd heard the thrumming in the pocket of his jacket. 'Your phone,' I said to Richard, looking over at him, surprised. 'Yeah,' he said, not answering it. He turned to look at me. 'Well,' he said, reaching for my hand, 'what do we do now?'

'Maybe seeing that surfing kid pull her son up out of the water like that made her know something,' Kath was saying. 'Something she didn't know before. And maybe this new thing just came sweeping through her like a great big wind. You know, like in the Bible; a *tempest,* isn't that what they call it?'

'Let's hear it for the Old Testament,' said Richard, raising his bottle.

For a moment I closed my eyes, then opened them again. Richard was looking at me. 'You ok, Mags?' he said.

I didn't say anything.

'And so this wind, this great big Bible wind, suddenly comes rushing through, lifting up everything in its way and flinging things all over the place. You can't control it; it just is. So she can't control this feeling she gets, this force; and it's so powerful. She ends up hitting her own son. It's not that she doesn't love him. If anything, it's that she loves him too much.' Kath picked up her beer. 'That's what I think, anyway,' she said.

I wanted to move my chair around to where Art was. He looked so sad sitting there, thinking about our son. I wanted to put my arm around him, or even just to put my hand on top of his and leave it there; I wanted to, or at least part of me did. But I couldn't.

'We should probably go,' Richard said, 'it's getting late.'

'Yeah,' said Kath, smiling at Art and me.

'What about you, Richard?' I said. 'Is that what this is, you and Kath? The great big, the great big wind?'

'I don't know, Mags,' Richard said. He gave a little shrug and then stood up. 'Maybe it is. Let's hope so.' He looked at Kath and handed her her bag.

'Yeah,' I said. Still sitting, I lifted my glass. 'Let's hope.'

I could see the taxi-driver glancing at us in the mirror. Once,

I thought, once might be alright. And it was just once; we never did this again, though I know Richard wanted to, and I almost would have too, especially right after Ray died. So I didn't pull my hand away; I could have, but I didn't. I sat there as the taxi sped towards our hotel, past the palm trees rustling in the breeze; and beyond, way out in the darkness, the sigh, rising and falling, of the sea.

INTO THE RED

I'd a picture on the wall of Tina with Sean, but I tore it down last week, after she told me she was leaving. Australia. 'There's nothing for me here,' she said. Sean was sitting on her knee in his Spiderman outfit, playing with an action-figure. 'What about me?' I said. 'I'm here, amn't I?' 'You're...' she said, and then she stopped, turning towards the window in the Visiting Area, and didn't say anymore. I started trying to explain again why I'd done it, but she just sighed. 'Don't start that shite again, Dean,' she said. Sean kept his head down the whole time, twisting the plastic arms and legs of the action-figure, punching and kicking whatever invisible enemy he could see.

I liked working in L & W in the old place, but even though the stock was walking out the door there was never enough room to store it all. So when Anto told us we'd be moving to a big new place out near Blossom Lodge, the estate they were just finishing building, it made sense. All those houses; and all those new customers looking for patio-heaters and picture hooks and garden furniture and God knows what. A huge barn of a place, it was. They promoted me to Assistant Manager, and took on a load of new staff, and that's how I met Tina. On opening day there was a big party in the new store. Anto had his picture taken with O'Leary the local TD, and some shiny suit from head office in England. Later a whole load of us went to the pub, and me and Tina ended up getting off with each other, and six months later we moved into an apartment out near the canal, me and Tina and Sean, Tina's little fella. The building society was falling over itself to give us a loan, especially after we'd shown them the letter from Anto explaining that the new house-owners would be moving in to Blossom Lodge any day now, once the planning thing was sorted. Then we'd all be able to sit back and watch the moolah come rolling in.

That's all they talk about in here, the screws: money. Over-time bans. Pay cuts. Lost allowances. I saw a couple of them on the landing the other day, comparing payslips. I'm on Special Obs, so every twenty minutes one of them is supposed to squint in the spyhole to make sure I haven't topped myself, or escaped, or whatever. But they couldn't be arsed. I could be in here swinging from the ceiling or digging a tunnel like yer man in the *Shawshank Redemption* and they wouldn't notice, unless it meant more money.

I bet one of them got a big wad of notes from whatever journo took my picture while I was playing football during exercise in the yard. *Face Of A Killer,* the headline said; Lanigan gave me a copy when he came in to talk about my appeal. He'd warned me before the trial, in fairness to him. 'If you plead guilty,' he'd said, 'with no previous, early plea, remorse, you'll get four, be out in three.' 'But he deserved it,' I'd said. Lanigan looked up then, startled. 'You can't say that, Dean.'

The window's so small and so high up it looks like a stamp at the top of a postcard. Below it I have all the newspaper cuttings I could get: photos, articles, opinion pieces, court reports. I've the whole wall nearly covered. They loved giving out about Milliken and all the others in StanCorp; well, now they've something else to give out about. *Our Broken Country: The Loss of Law and Order,* one piece trumpeted. But this place was banjaxed long before the thing with me and Milliken. And the ones mourning him now never stopped giving out about him and StanCorp. StanCorp wasn't even its real name; it was Standard Corporate Bank. But Milliken always called it StanCorp, and that's what was on the baseball hats and umbrellas and mobile phone covers: StanCorp, with underneath the logo of an eagle, its wings spread wide. Pat Kenny and the rest of them nearly burst their shite laughing at that eagle when the bank went bust. *StanCorp chickens come home to roost.* They wanted this. They stirred it up so that the whole country hated StanCorp and Milliken, and now they're giving out because someone actually did something about it. But if it hadn't been me it would have been somebody else.

Anto looked pretty shook when he called us in to the warehouse. We all just stood there while he read the announcement. The union woman asked a couple of questions but no one was really listening. 'With immediate effect.' 'Enormous regret.' 'Fully committed to Ireland.' 'No option but to close.' There were TV cameras outside already as we drove out past the entrance to Blossom Lodge, past all those nearly-built houses with weeds growing in their front gardens and the roads fenced off by the receiver. It wasn't planning permission that had been the problem; it was money. The builder was living in Spain. Even the other banks were broke now, thanks to StanCorp apparently. A few months later, after we'd missed a second payment, we were sitting on two plastic chairs in the building society, Tina and me, opposite O'Leary the TD's brother, Willie. *Relationship Advisor*, the sign on the desk said. Willie was looking at us with his fingers joined under the tip of his nose, like he was a priest. He kept picking up and putting down a page of figures. 'This can't go on,' he said. 'Sure, I know it can't,' I said, 'but what d'ya expect us to do? There's no work out there at the moment.' I could feel my cheeks getting hot, and Tina was shushing me, trying to calm me down. But Willie just sat there, shaking his head. 'Something has to be done,' he said.

Apparently I have 'schizophrenic/suicidal ideations'. This fella Dunne has been in to see me a couple of times. I don't know whether he's a counsellor or a shrink or what, but I heard him say to one of the screws that Dundrum might be a better place for me. I've told him I'm not psycho, though; I keep trying to explain but he won't listen. 'I'm not saying I set out to kill him,' I said. 'But he got what was due to him; and the way it's worked out, wasn't it for the best?' Dunne sucked on the top of his pen and wrote on his file. They'd never have convicted him anyway, Milliken. Look at all those scumbags walking in and out of Dublin Castle during the tribunals, strutting up and down as if they'd done nothing wrong. Not one of them inside. Milliken would have got off, no doubt about it. Some guard would have dropped the ball in the witness box, or else the jury would just have given up. And he'd have been there, smiling and giving the thumbs up to the cameras as he left court after. Free.

'A vigilante, isn't that how you saw yourself?' He'd a big Shrek head on him, the prosecuting counsel, and he stood there with one foot up on the cushion of the bench, and a finger in the pocket of his waistcoat. 'You decided you'd take the law into your own hands, isn't that right?' he said. He was really enjoying himself now, Shrek was; he kept looking over at the jury for support. I could see Lanigan mouthing 'No, no,' at me. I said nothing. 'Ah, c'mon now, sir,' said Shrek, his jowls quivering indignantly. There was a little soup-stain on his gown. 'Are you going to answer me?' *An accident,* I'd agreed I'd say, after talking to Lanigan.

I had no desire to kill or injure the deceased. Lanigan had still wanted me to plead, right up to the end; he told me to say as little as possible if I gave evidence. He even wrote it out for me: *I never meant for this to happen.* But as I looked out at the jury staring back at me, and the judge scribbling away in her notepad, and Milliken's wife with his son beside her holding her hand, and Tina wiping her eyes, I realised what Lanigan had told me to say wasn't true. I never wanted courts, or a trial, or prison. But I didn't want what I had before all this, which was a big black sack of nothing. No money, no job, no apartment (very soon); nothing. And all of it Milliken's fault. Isn't that what they were all saying, the papers, the TV, the radio, online, everyone; that this entire mess was all down to Milliken, and that bank? At least this way — even if it hadn't turned out the way I'd expected — at least this way I had *something.* Milliken was gone, and never coming back, and I'd done that. A hero, one person on Twitter had called me. I liked the way that sounded.

He'd been coming out after a remand hearing. There'd still been no date fixed for his trial; the judge had spluttered about delays and the prosecution counsel had been huffing and puffing about the need for 'extra resources'. There were a couple of cameras outside the courthouse as he walked towards the car waiting for him at the bottom of the steps. His solicitor was beside him, carrying a big black brief case, looking importantly into the middle distance. Two guards were kicking their heels just inside the courthouse door; the Garda union boss said later this 'tragic incident' was 'an inevitable result of Government cutbacks on security and crime prevention'. There was an aul fella in a big white beard who looked like Santa, carrying a placard which read *Show Me The Money*, and a couple of his hangers-on. And me. I'd a tin of paint with me; it'd been on special offer in L&W the week before we closed. *Into the Red*, it was called; it seemed kind of appropriate. One of Santa's helpers started jeering Milliken as he came down the steps. 'Where's the money, Milliken?' he said. Milliken ignored him, looking straight ahead, but he had that smarmy grin you see in all the papers. I watched as he went past me, the dark blue suit and the gold bracelet and the ring of short blond curls like a crown. 'Fuck you, Milliken,' I said, almost to myself; he was nearly at the car. Then I swung the tin at him. The idea was the paint would empty out all over him; I'd loosened the lid beforehand. But instead the tin hit him on the side of the head, and he stumbled and went down. There was a crack as his head hit the bottom step. I lost hold of the tin, the lid finally coming off as it hit the ground. Bright red paint poured over the step. His solicitor went down on his knees to see if he was alright, but Milliken didn't move. Santa and his helpers started hooting and cheering, and then the guards grabbed me. They twisted my arms up behind my back, and one of them started calling into a walkie-talkie on his shoulder for an ambulance, and a squad car. The other one holding me was younger; he didn't say much, but when I saw his face I could tell it was the first time he'd seen anything like this. Cameras started flashing and clicking at Milliken on the step. And then the cameras turned around and pointed at me.

Superman. Batman. Spiderman. Sean had all the outfits.
He'd wear one everywhere he went with Tina and me; the
cinema, the park, even the beach. All those superheroes.
They protect the innocent and make sure the guilty
are brought to justice. Isn't that what I did? It wasn't
just Twitter or the Facebook campaign trying to get me
released. People started daubing red paint outside the
offices of StanCorp and other banks; they even did it
outside a couple of Government Departments. Two women
were arrested for trying to paint the gates of Leinster
House. The Minister for Justice came on television. 'We
must never, never take the law into our own hands, no
matter how strongly we feel about what has happened to
our economy,' he said. He sounded just like Shrek did later,
at the end of the trial, when he was telling the jury they
had to convict me, thumping his pudgy fist into his hand
as he went on about the law of the land and the law of the
jungle. It didn't take them long to decide anyway, despite
Lanigan's brave last-ditch effort to have me declared unfit
to continue trial by reason of being mute 'by visitation of
God'. Nine years. Lanigan pursed his lips when the judge
announced her sentence. But after the verdict Mrs Milliken
gave evidence about her husband and what his death meant
to her and the family. And she said it was a consolation to
her that someone else's life would be made better by his
death. I didn't know what she meant, but Lanigan explained
it later; it was in the Victim Impact Report. Milliken had
been young (too young to be head of a bank, some said)
and healthy, and he'd had an Organ Donor Card. When
they'd switched off the machines a few days after what

happened, the doctors were able to take one of his kidneys ('harvesting,' I think it's called) and transplant it into a woman who'd been ill for years. I never found out who she was, or how she was chosen to receive Milliken's last gift. But as the cell door closed that evening, I was thinking: if I hadn't done what I did, that woman would probably soon be dead. So as well as everything else, what I had done had saved that woman's life.

When Visiting Time ended Tina stood up, lifting Sean off her lap onto the ground. He looked quickly at me and then at Tina. 'Will Dean be going to Australia as well, Mammy?' 'No, love,' she said, avoiding my eyes, 'Dean's going to be staying here for a while.' She stepped back so that I couldn't hug her or give her a kiss. 'See ya, Dean,' she said. I could see Dunne at the door of the Visiting Area with a file under his arm, waiting to talk to her. 'Bye, Dean,' Sean said as he took her hand. Then the two of them walked away.

I've been having this dream lately. I told Dunne about it when he came to see me last. He's the top of the pen near chewed off by now, but he writes it down anyway. I am flying over the city, a scarlet cape streaming in my wake. It's night, but I can see everything clearly; L & W, and Blossom Lodge, and our apartment and the canal. I can see the TV studios and the hospital, and the newspapers offices and the Dáil, and the courthouse; and up the river the Financial Centre, with the offices of StanCorp and the other banks standing empty, abandoned. As I fly I gaze down at the sleeping city, looking for people to save, and people to punish; and I know that the buildings of those who deserve to be punished are marked with a daub of wet paint. I soar over the city, searching and searching. But I can't find anyone to save. The whole city is painted red.

THE TRUCK-DRIVER'S WIFE

I hand him his school bag, but still he won't let go. He presses against my waist. His father's eyes, looking up at me.

'Please,' he says, 'please Maman, no.'

Clingy: always was, even before.

Other mothers are looking at us but I don't look back. I don't know any of them.

The bell rings. Children begin hosting towards the school's front door.

'Go on, Oscar,' I say, prising his arms from me.

He backs away slowly; then, still watching me, he starts trudging towards the entrance.

'Bye,' I say, and I give a little wave.

When he sees me waving he stops. He doesn't wave back; he just stops and looks at me.

'C'mon, Oscar,' says the teacher in the doorway. She nods at me as she ushers him inside.

Four weeks since he started. Here.

'Good boy, Oscar,' I say. The door shuts.

I turn around. The yard is empty, the other mothers gone.

There's no one else in Café Francine. Next door is Lexi's, a grubby convenience store with dead flies and ancient tinsel in the window. The unit on the other side is vacant.

I thought he'd want to meet in the apartment, but Chavez prefers the café.

'You should try one of these,' he says, wiping a flake of pastry from his mouth.

'No thanks,' I say.

He has violet lips, Chavez, and a brown leather jacket which barely closes.

'Seriously,' he says. His stumpy fingers tear off another piece of the Danish. 'You don't know what you're missing.'

Our second meeting. *'Once a fortnight,'* the Department memo says, *'you will meet your Programme Liaison Officer.'*

'So,' says Chavez, raising a finger at Francine behind the counter, pointing at his cup. 'How's everything? How's…?'

'Oscar,' I say.

'Oscar, yes.'

Francine lumbers over, smiles and fills his cup. She offers me some more, but I decline.

'Well,' says Chavez, 'how is Oscar getting on?'

I think of Oscar's questions — about how long we are staying here, and when we can go home, and where his Papa is. I look down at my shoes.

'So-so,' I say.

I turn my empty cup around in its saucer, slowly, like a clock.

'The school,' I say. 'He doesn't like the school.'

'Good school,' Chavez says, rounding up crumbs on his plate. 'He'll be fine, but it takes time. Always does.'

He dabs his lips with his serviette, sits back.

'And you, Isolde.' His eyebrows furrow slightly as he says it, my name: my new, Programme name. 'How are *you*?'

Back in the apartment I wash our breakfast dishes: Oscar's bowl, and mug, and plate, and spoon, and knife. My juice-glass. Then I wipe the table. It's clean, but I scrub it anyway, up and down, up and down. A pine veneer, not like the solid oak in our old kitchen, back in Paris. This one's rickety, and pale. Cheap. It came with the apartment; it was waiting for us here when we arrived.

I take out the pad of notepaper, and a pen. The pen's a Bic, but the notepaper's creamy, sky-blue, thick; the envelopes are the same. I want each letter to look nice for my husband, even though he will never see them.

I sit down at the table. I open the pad at a new page, and start to write.

His name first. 'Dear Yossie,' I begin.

Mid-morning a few days later, a knock on the door.

'The fisheye,' Chavez says, *'always use the fisheye, and if you've any doubts, don't answer.'*

But I know, even without looking through the fisheye, who it is.

'Bloody lift's broken again,' Marianne says. Marianne lives across the corridor, and when I open the door she's standing there with two bags of shopping and a cigarette dangling from her lips.

'Jesus, Isolde. So *clean*. You OCD or something?' she says, peering inside.

Yossie would've liked Marianne. She's blonde, the way I was before I came here; before I cut and dyed my hair. Older than me, but not much. Curvy; just Yossie's type, though Yossie liked lots of different women, and lots of them liked him. Which is what I thought of first, when I found out about the Monday nights.

'You want to come over?' she says.

In Marianne's apartment there are clothes on hangers hooked on bookshelves, and ashtrays filled to the brim, and magazines.

'Coffee?' Marianne says. 'Something stronger?'

'Just…juice,' I say. She purrs mock-approvingly, and winks as she splashes something extra, something clear, into her coffee cup.

'So,' she says, pushing some newspapers off the couch as she sits down, 'what's new?'

'*We've checked her out,*' Chavez says, '*nothing to worry about.*'

'Oh, nothing,' I say. 'Oscar's still not happy in the school.'

Marianne takes a gulp from her cup. 'Miss his Papa, does he?'

I look at my glass.

'Yeah, maybe,' I say. I take a sip, but I don't look up. It's some sort of fruit juice; warm, and sweet.

Marianne leans in. 'Poor thing,' she says. 'But he is only....'

'Five,' I say.

'Five. He's *young*,' she says. 'And anyway, you had to leave, Isolde, after what Marc did to you. The bastard.'

'Your husband's name is Marc,' the memo from the Department says, 'and you left him because he started beating you.'

'I know. You're right,' I say, although it doesn't feel right. Because even though it sounds ridiculous now to say it, Yossie was not a violent man.

She puts her hand on my arm. 'Ah look, I'm sorry. I didn't mean to upset you. Here, give me that.'

She takes my glass over to the counter, unscrews the cap of whatever bottle she's been using, and pours two splashes in. Then she hands me back the glass and sits down again, closer this time. 'Now, try this,' she says.

I take a sip. God, it's strong.

Marianne lights another cigarette. 'Plenty more fish in the sea,' she says, 'especially for a girl like you.'

I smile back weakly. 'What about *you*?' I say.

'Oh, I've had it with men,' she says, taking a drag. Marianne's husband—what did she say his name was?— left two years ago. 'Finished. Good riddance to them!' She raises her cup: a toast.

'Yeah,' I say. I tilt my glass half-heartedly towards her.

She takes a drink, squinting at me. A tendril of cigarette

smoke rises from her hand. 'But you,' she says, smirking, 'what's this *you've* been up to?'

'What do you mean?' I say.

'Oh, I know your little secret,' she says, and she taps the side of her nose.

'The apartment block has been pre-approved for Programme use by the Department. All residents have been vetted.'

'What secret?' I say, wondering if she can detect the flutter in my voice.

Marianne smirks again. 'I know,' she says. 'I *know.*'

Is she drunk? Maybe she's drunk.

'What?' I say. 'Know what?'

Marianne jiggles her cup playfully at me. 'A little bird told me,' she says. 'About you-know-who.' She grins.

'Who?' I ask her. *Calm Juliette, calm.*

'I know all about you,' she says in a sing-song voice. She refills her cup and plonks herself back down beside me, waving her finger like the conductor of a tiny orchestra. 'I know all about—'

'Know *what*?' I say again.

And suddenly she stops. Because I'm shouting, shouting at Marianne.

She looks at me curiously, alarmed. I can hear the thrum and gurgle of the washing-machine in the kitchen.

'Francine,' she says eventually. 'Francine told me about your date. The other day. In the café.'

I think of Chavez, licking his lips, smoothing back his thinning hair.

'Oh, *him*,' I say. 'He's...he's nothing.' I shake my head

and smile at her, trying to make up.

Marianne smiles back mirthlessly.

'He's just...it doesn't matter. Honestly.' I grimace an apology. 'Listen, I didn't mean to...'

'It's ok,' Marianne says.

But it is not ok.

'Well,' she says, standing up, 'you've lots of things to do, I'm sure.'

Fides. That's what the crest said, on the jersey of his favourite team. *Faithful*.

About three months ago, Yossie came home saying that the depot had organised an indoor football game for Monday nights. So I dug out that replica jersey he'd had for years, and a pair of shorts and football socks, and a pair of runners; I packed them into a kitbag on Sunday night and left it by the front door.

The morning after the game when I went to wash it, the gear was spotless. No stains, no perspiration, no smell.

The next week, and the week after that, the same: the runners and the shorts and socks lying there in the bag, exactly as I'd left them, the jersey neatly folded on top. So of course I started wondering what he was at, and with whom.

Faithful. People think 'truck-driver', they think a fat slob, sitting on his arse up in the cab, munching all-day breakfast rolls. But Yossie wasn't like that. He wasn't tall, but he was trim and well-built, with lovely arms; toned, muscular arms that I knew plenty of women would love to have wrapped round them. I sniffed him once or twice when he came home, in case I'd smell her off him. The other woman: I was convinced that he was sleeping with someone else, that he was being unfaithful. But he wasn't. Although I only know that now.

There's a park not far from the apartment. We go there on Saturdays. We walk along cracked pavements, passing window after window with a sign that says 'For Sale'.

In the park there is a play-area with swings, and climbing frames, and a slide. Oscar likes the slide.

Teenage boys perch on the benches, their hoodies up even though it is almost summer: three, four, five of them.

One says something: the others laugh and look at me.

Oscar stands at the top of the slide. 'Alright now, Maman? Alright to come down?'

'Yes,' I say, 'yes, it's alright now.'

He sits down, but instead of allowing himself glide, he bum-shuffles his way to the bottom, clutching the edge on either side.

'Let go,' I say, 'let go, Oscar. You'll be fine.'

One of the hoodies laughs again.

Twelve of them, uniformed and armed, searched the house.

I was sitting at the table in the kitchen, opposite Cendron and Blanc.

'This…this is not my husband,' I said.

'Jesus Christ,' said Blanc, slamming the table. He turned to his inspector. 'We've enough on her already,

Madame, why don't we just take her in?'

Cendron raised her hand. 'Hold on a minute,' she said.

She leaned across the table towards me. Hair the colour of ash. No wedding ring.

'Juliette,' she said, 'You need to help us. Because if you —'

'I don't know anything,' I said, 'I already told you, I don't know.'

There were four photos on the table, screen-grabs from traffic cameras of the truck making its way through the streets, heading for the market square. Blanc jabbed at one of them; a close-up, of the driver. 'There, see. That's him; that's your husband, Iosef, yes?'

I looked again. It was Yossie alright, but it didn't make sense. None of this made sense.

'You don't understand,' I said.

Blanc rolled his eyes and thumped the oak again. 'No, *you* don't understand!' He pulled out another, thicker, file of pictures and began to lay them out, one by one, facing me.

'Look!' he said, his face almost touching mine; I could smell his coffee-breath.

'This is what your husband did,' he said. 'This, and this, and this.'

I looked down. The pictures were of women, mostly, but men as well. And children; there must have been ten, twelve children.

'Juliette,' said Cendron.

Thirty-nine pictures, covering the entire table.

'Juliette,' Cendron said, again. 'You have to think of Oscar now. Because if you don't help us, we'll have to take you in.'

I glanced towards the front room; Oscar's voice, and the voice of the officer who was in there with him.

'And if we have to take you into custody,' continued Cendron, 'I don't know when you'll be next able to see him.'

My eyes began to fill.

'So, come on now, Juliette,' said Cendron. A level tone, with just a woodnote of irritation. 'The morning, yesterday, before Iosef...before he left, what did you talk about? What did he say?'

There were voices chattering beyond the front door. A white light suddenly lit up the outside of the house. I looked inquiringly at Cendron.

'Arclights,' Blanc said. 'For the TV cameras. You're famous, Juliette. Congratulations.'

'And if you help us,' Cendron continued, 'we'll make sure that you'll be safe. You and Oscar.'

I swallowed. 'He...after Oscar'd gone to school, I made him breakfast.'

Neither of them spoke.

'He said then that the run was down to Naples, and that he'd be back late tomorrow.'

Cendron made a note and nodded. 'Naples. OK. What else?'

'He said to make sure Oscar stayed back afterwards in school, for football. He likes football, Yossie.' *Liked.* 'He knew Oscar wasn't keen.'

'Football.' Cendron shifted slightly in her chair. 'You said before that Iosef—that Yossie told you he played football Monday nights?'

I could feel the heat rising in my cheeks.

'I promise you,' I said, 'I never knew. Those meetings you mentioned earlier, with the others; he never said anything. I never knew he was…'

Involved. But not with someone else, at least that. And although what he'd done was worse, far worse, this small fact, that he'd been faithful, was for me a kind of consolation.

'What else, Juliette?' Cendron was losing patience. 'What else did he say?'

'He said…we said goodbye, and then he left.'

I'd been at the sink washing dishes. He'd come over, put his arm around my waist, and kissed me lightly on the lips. 'Bye, Jules,' he'd said. Nothing ominous; just the casual tenderness of an ordinary marriage.

And I wanted to tell them — though I didn't — that this was not the kiss of a man who an hour later would drive a truck loaded with explosives into a crowded market square; who, when the truck finally came to a halt among the stalls of cheese and fruit and fish laid out on ice, would then lean back calmly in the driver's seat and press the button. The man who kissed me was not that man.

'Dear Yossie,' I write, and then I stop. Always: what else would I say?

I motion to him to lift his arms so I can put his pyjama top on, and he does. He's getting better, but he's not happy. 'I don't like it here,' he keeps saying.

I want to tell him that I do not want to live in this place either, with its boarded-up shops and hooded youths and a wind that tastes of dust. But instead I say, 'You'll get to like it, Oscar, honestly.'

I pull the duvet up tight around him. He moves over and pats the space he's made. I lie down beside him. 'Maman, when will I see Papa?' he says.

I want to press my face against his little bony shoulder and weep. But instead I say, 'Not for a long time.'

'How long?' he asks.

'A long, long time,' I say. 'Maybe never.'

He turns away.

'Don't be sad, Oscar.'

His shoulders are trembling; little angry sobs...

'You're wrong,' he says, his back still to me.

'Oscar, please,' I say, but it's no use.

'You're wrong, Maman. I *hate* you.' His breath coming in short, hot bursts. 'I *will* see Papa, I will.'

And I am. Wrong. Three weeks later, we're in Lexi's. 'Wait over at the door,' I say, and I head down the back to the shelves of bruised apples and wilting lettuces and potatoes sprouting tumours.

The bell over the door tinkles.

I pick out three wizened oranges. 'Maman, Maman, look!' I hear Oscar calling. He doesn't sound frightened or alarmed; if anything, he sounds excited.

'What is it, Oscar?' I say.

'Look, Maman,' he says, 'it's Papa!'

For a moment I freeze. Then I stuff the oranges into my basket and trot back towards the front of the shop, thinking that I should have made it clear; I should have explained what 'dead' really means.

Lexi's at the till, with his silver tooth and his permanent three-day beard; and Francine, who's just come in, is leaning on the counter. They're both staring at Oscar who's at the rack of magazines, pointing. *Massacre: We Remember*, one says, with a picture of the market square covered in flowers and furry toys and candles on the cover; and in the right-hand corner, under the words *Suicide Bomber* a photo — an old one, but it's definitely Yossie, it's definitely him.

'See Maman? See?' says Oscar. And he points again so proudly at his father, and looks at me, and smiles.

AFTER PANDORA

The turtle was small; it must have lost contact with its mother. Bud was leaning out over the side, holding on to one of its flippers. He was trying to haul it aboard, but the turtle kept twisting and nipping at his fingers.

'Give us a hand here, Dean, would you?' he said.

I shuffled over to the opening to help, but when I did the life raft started to list.

'Hey, Sam,' I said, 'trim her, will you?' She was so far over that water was coming in; it felt like she might capsize.

'Sam!' I said again. All the boy had to do was shift himself to the opposite side, for balance. But he just lay there groaning, and I had to slide back in and leave Bud to it.

Somehow Bud got a hand on the turtle's other flipper and

managed to drag it into the life raft. It lay on its shell wriggling and snapping, its little old man's head turning from side to side. Bud slumped back under the canopy. The side-walls of the life raft sagged with his weight; the tubes needed pumping again, and it was Bud's turn, but I didn't say this.

'Right, Dean,' said Bud, nodding at the turtle, 'hold this guy down, and give us the knife.'

The knife was hanging on a lanyard from the canopy. It had a marlin-spike, a shackle-key, and a blade. I untied it and handed it to Bud, and then I kneeled over the turtle, pinning down its flippers with my knees while Bud opened the blade.

'Bailer,' Bud said. 'Hold the bailer underneath, for the blood.'

I manoeuvred the plastic scoop into position as Bud began to cut across the turtle's neck. Some oozed out immediately, though not as much as I'd expected. It looked a bit like wine, swilling darkly at the bottom of the bailer, and it tasted sour, resinous, but I swallowed some anyway. So did Bud.

There was a little bit left, and I pressed the bailer to Sam's lips, trying to pour it in. He lifted his hand to hold the bailer, but the blood just dribbled out the side of his mouth.

'You're wasting it,' Bud said.

He sliced the turtle-meat into strips, and hung them from the top of the canopy to keep them dry. The stink made me retch, but it didn't stop me eating when my turn came, gnawing as long as possible on each piece.

That was the fourth day when we caught the turtle. We never caught another after that; we never even caught a fish. There was supposed to be a fishing line in the emergency bag, but when we opened it the line was missing. We could see them gliding nearby, dorados mostly; sometimes they'd thump the underside of the life raft, hard. I tried leaning out, with Bud holding my legs, to see if I could catch one with the orange-net, but they were so clever and so quick, weaving and diving, all blues and violets and greens, like swerving stained-glass windows. We had long since cut up the Mars bars and shared them out. Same with the oranges. One day there was rain, a short shower: we held the bailer up even though it still had some turtle blood inside, and managed to catch a little bit; a couple of mouthfuls each. By the fifteenth day we had nothing.

Sam was Golding's son. Bud hadn't been sure about him coming along, but Golding had insisted, and Golding was paying. 'Your call,' Bud said, 'but he's your responsibility.' 'He'll be fine,' Golding replied, 'he's a good sailor. Aren't you?' he said, grinning at his son. 'Suppose,' Sam mumbled, in that 14-year-old way that sounds surly, but isn't. 'Sure you are,' said Golding, punching him playfully on the shoulder. He *was* good too, skipping around the foredeck, and yanking up the spinnaker so fast that Golding could hardly keep up with him as he tailed the halyard on the winch and Ballantyne wound back the sheet. They were both dead now, Golding and Ballantyne, and it was just Bud and Sam. And me.

She wasn't quick, *Pandora*, but she was comfortable, especially down below. Golding told us he'd always had this dream of buying a boat and sailing round the world, even before he sold whatever dotcom thing it was he'd made his money on. We left the Galapagos on the 5th, expecting to reach the Marquesas by the 28th. The night of the 6th was warm; there was a bit of a sea, but not much. Golding was below in his bunk, asleep. So was Ballantyne, Golding's pal from the City who'd never set foot on a boat before. Bud and I were on watch, and Sam. Like I said, he was a good kid: lots of guys his age would sleep the whole way through a trip like this, but he did his bit, and was keen to learn. Coming up at the start of the watch, he'd brought a bag of baby Mars bars from the galley, and a net of oranges; and because we were having a sing-song up on deck, Golding had told him to put the washboards in and close the hatch, so he and Ballantyne could sleep.

Maybe it was the singing that attracted them; or maybe it was the shape of *Pandora*'s hull from below, ploughing through the waves. I'd seen them before, but it was Sam's first time. 'Whales!' he said, pointing over the port side, and then to starboard. A dozen or more surged along on either side of us in the moonlit foam, one or two occasionally surfacing to blow. 'Cool,' Sam said, transfixed. For a moment the only sound was the rush of the wind, and the gurgle and hiss of the sea. Then there was a thud underneath us and suddenly *Pandora* was on her ear, lee-rail in the waves and water pouring in through the hull. 'The keel,' yelled Bud; already he'd pulled a knife from his sailing jacket and leapt up to slash the lines that held the life raft on deck amidships. 'Keel's gone.' One of the whales must have misjudged it; just got a bit too close, I guess. Bud lashed a line from the life raft to the boat's stern-rail and hurled the life raft over the back of the boat. At least it inflated quickly. 'Jump!' Bud said to Sam, and he did. He was still holding the bag of Mars bars as he landed on the life raft, half-in, half-out. Bud cut the main and spinnaker halyards in the hope *Pandora* might right herself, but it was too late; even in the cockpit, we were already up to our chests in water.

I could hear Sam whimpering from the life raft. 'Dad,' he kept saying, 'what about Dad?' 'You'd better get in too,' Bud said to me, so I jumped. He stayed on board for as long as he could, trying to force open the cabin-hatch, but by now the water was up to his neck, and I was afraid *Pandora* would take the life raft down with her. Sam was still mewling under the canopy beside me. 'C'mon, Bud!' I shouted. Bud looked at me. He gave the hatch one more go but it was no use. Then he cut the line tied to the stern-rail and swam out to the life raft, which had already started drifting away. He'd managed to grab the net of oranges; they thumped and splashed in the water as he swam. When he reached the life raft he threw them inside, pulled himself up and eventually clambered in. The last we saw of *Pandora* was her crosstrees, sinking like a crucifix beneath the waves. The whales, powering on through the night, were gone.

Bud was certain we would die. He'd written his wife a note on the back of the instruction booklet for the flares, with a pencil he'd found in the pocket of his shorts. *Dear Annie*, it said, *By the time you get this you'll know I'm gone. We all are. I love you. Take care of Simon and Sean and Lizzie. Love, Bud.* Bud's brief said this note was helpful, because it showed he'd really believed we were finished.

My own brief told me just to keep my trap shut. 'They've no witnesses,' she said, 'and they can't make you give evidence.'

'Would I not be better off if I'd written a note as well?' I asked.

'That depends,' she replied, regarding me evenly. Parker, her name is. She's small and blonde, fresh-faced; a bit young-looking to be handling a case like this, if you ask me, but the solicitor said she was good.

'Bud's note is fine, as far as it goes,' she said, 'but it doesn't say anything about the other thing you told me. About casting lots.'

He was so much younger than the two of us: I don't know why Sam went downhill so fast. Maybe those rolls of fat Bud and I were carrying round our waists meant it took longer for our bodies to start feasting on our organs. Or maybe it was the shock of his Dad dying. We tried to get him to help us catch some fish but he wasn't up to it. Soon he wasn't able to take his turn pumping up the tubes. I even fed him once, inserting a strip of turtle-meat on the marlin spike between his lips. For a moment the piece of flesh lay motionless in his mouth, the way Father Redmond in school had told us the host should lie immediately after Communion. I could hear Bud growling as he watched: he sat up, and for a moment I thought he was going to come over and take the morsel out of Sam's mouth, until Sam very slowly began to chew. By the eighteenth day Sam's lips were covered in sores and one of his eyes was almost completely closed.

A shoulder of ham, glazed, I remember; that was the first dream, before the other dreams started. The sweet aroma of those cloves as well, stuck all over it. And carrots; even though I didn't really like carrots I could see them, vivid orange with salty butter brightly running off. Potatoes too, roasted bronze in goose fat, and a creamy parsley sauce.

I asked Bud if he ever dreamed of food.

'A burger,' he said, 'with onion rings, and relish. And a cone of chips, sprinkled with salt.'

'You, Sam?' I said.

His lips moved slightly, although by then he could hardly speak.

'Ice cream.' At least, I think that's what he said.

We'd been talking about wives; wives and children. Bud met Annie at a friend's wedding; he'd known immediately she was the one. They'd started having kids straight away; eight and six and four, they were now, and though he didn't see as much of them as he wanted because he spent so much time away on boats, he really, really loved them. Louise and I'd met in a bar. She was willowy and dark and sassy; still is. Our daughter Sally is the image of her. Louise hated the water, so when we got together, I gave up sailing. Swallowed the anchor. But three months ago, after I lost my job, Bud persuaded me to come back, to help him with the delivery of this new yacht, *Pandora*. 'Go if you want,' Louise said, 'I don't care.' We'd been having problems for a while, and not just because I was out of work. 'You're not the man I married,' she said to me one night. 'It's you who's changed, Louise,' I said back, 'not me.' Though maybe both of us were right.

I'm not even sure why I was telling Bud all this. But after I'd finished Bud looked over at Sam, who was asleep. Then he reached down into the life raft's emergency bag. Half the stuff that was supposed to be in there was missing; there were just flares and a torch, and rolls of bandages and a box of matches. We'd used the bandages to cover some of the sores we had from lying in one place the whole time. The flares were in case we saw a ship. The matches, though, were useless; the sulphur heads kept flaking off. So when Bud opened the match-box and took out three of them I didn't know what he was at. He broke a bit off one, and then held the three together in his fist. He nodded towards Sam and then looked at me.

'For Sally,' he said, waggling the matches at me. 'For Sally and Louise. You owe it to them.'

I started to reach out, and then I stopped.

'Come on,' Bud said. 'At least this way, two of us will have a chance.'

I could see the broken match, sticking out at an angle. So could Bud. But I couldn't do it. Not because I wasn't hungry, or because I knew the result, but because I was afraid.

'You have to,' said Bud.

I shook my head and pushed his hand away. Bud slumped back against the inside of the life raft. The tubes had gone soft again: they needed pumping, and even though it was Bud's turn, I dragged the nozzle over and pushed it in, and started to pump.

'Afraid?' asked Parker. Her pen was poised, mid-air. 'What do you mean, afraid, Dean?'

I shrugged. 'I don't know.'

'Did you think you would die?' she said.

'Yeah, yeah, of course.'

'So what were you afraid of then?'

Even though it made no sense at all, I could hear him, hear his voice.

'And what, boys, is the name of the last sacrament?' Father Redmond was strolling between the rows of desks.

'Anybody?' he asked. I could even smell him in the dream, a whiff of Gold Flake and the faint hint of talcum powder as he wafted past. Outside the wind hammered against our classroom windows. I looked around to see who knew the answer. Every single desk was occupied by an enormous dorado.

'The Sacrament of the Sick,' said Father Redmond, 'the sacrament, usually, of the dying.' He licked his lips. 'Also known as Last Rites, or Extreme Unction.'

I could hear splashing when I woke. They were both leaning out over the side, Sam further out than Bud; maybe, I thought, they've caught something at last.

'What is it?' I said. I tried to clamber over towards them, but the life raft began to tip. Sam fell back inside. He was retching and moaning, his eyes rolling in his head.

'Seawater,' said Bud. He was holding on to Sam by his frayed shirt collar. 'He's been drinking seawater.'

He let go of Sam and flopped down on to the floor. And then he sat up, his hand raised, pointing out to sea.

'Ship,' he said. 'I'm telling you, a ship.'

He started shouting then, and waving his arms. 'Over here!' he kept saying. I tried to follow what Bud was looking at, but one of my own eyes was starting to close by then, and I couldn't see too much. I started shouting as well, though, just in case.

'Get the flares,' he shouted. I handed one to him and he pulled the tag. The flare hissed as it shot into the air; it was late afternoon, and soon we could hardly see it against the blinding sky, high above us like a faint pink smoky star. 'Another one,' he said. He pulled its tag and the second one rose over our heads. By now Sam had passed out. 'Again,' said Bud. 'Last one,' I warned, but he just grabbed it and let it off. We roared and screamed and waved, myself and Bud, but nothing happened; no looming shape, no low thrum of an approaching engine.

'Bastards,' Bud said eventually to the empty horizon. 'You bastards.' He sunk to his knees, covering his face with his hands: he was crying, or trying to cry, except no tears would come. I squinted out again over the ocean, but I still couldn't see anything.

Parker looked at me.

'And then...?' she said.

I lowered my head and said nothing.

She cleared her throat. 'You just did what you had to,' she said.

'Did I?' I said.

'In an emergency, though, a whispered Act of Contrition will be enough.'

Father Redmond was leaning back against the side-wall of the life raft; the tubes had gone soft again, but I couldn't remember whose turn it was.

I undid the lanyard and took the knife down from the canopy, clicking the blade into the open position.

'Here,' I said, handing Bud the bailer.

Underneath the life raft the sea rippled and rolled.

I scooched over to where Sam was lying and put my mouth up beside his ear; I could smell his fetid breath, his filthy matted hair.

'Sam,' I said, shaking him gently. His eyes flickered.

'Sam, I...'

His lips moved, very slightly. 'Me?' he said.

'Yes, Sam,' I said.

Bud held the bailer up at Sam's chest.

Father Redmond's voice was grave. His shiny, polished shoes caught the light. 'And *in extremis*, you may say it for him. The deceased.'

I laid the knife against Sam's throat just below his Adam's apple, then slowly turned it up so that the edge was against the skin.

And I started to recite. 'Oh my God, I am heartily sorry for having offended thee.' There was a small mottle of rust at one end of the blade.

'The hearing,' Father Redmond was saying from the far side of the life raft, his mahogany-stained smoker's finger tapping his ear, 'of all the senses, the hearing is the last to go.'

ALMOST THE SAME BLUE

You recognise it immediately, the imitation-silver teddy bear dangling from its cheap chain. There is a torn scrap of paper in the envelope as well, an unknown phone number scrawled in biro.

'Please, no, Olivia,' says Donald when you tell him.

'But you insisted we should follow up on everything,' you say to him, the man who'd been your husband when it happened, almost two years ago. '*No stone unturned*, remember? You *said*.'

There is a silence on the other end of the phone. 'She's gone, Olivia,' Donald says eventually. You imagine him slowly shaking his head. 'You need to learn to grieve,' he says. You hang up, and weigh the pendant in your hand, thinking that to grieve would be a kind of treason, and although Donald has suggested that you contact the police about the envelope, you know you will not go back to the airless torpor of the station, the weary face of Lehane, the heavy-set detective who said six months ago that scarce resources meant the investigation was being scaled back.

So you tell no one else, although you ring the number, just in case, and when it eventually rings out you are almost relieved.

But the second time it answers.

The new notes come slickly from the machines. Twelve withdrawals, twelve different ATMs: it takes three days, but this is how he wants it, the voice who gives you the instructions in almost-perfect English. You say her name and ask to speak to her, and you hear him shouting in another language to someone else, wherever he is answering your call, before he replies: 'Right now that is not possible, but soon.' You ask is she alright, your heart lunging in your chest. 'Yes, yes,' he says impatiently, and then he talks again about the money, and where and when he'll meet you.

'And no police, yes?' he says, and for a moment the jumbled syntax confuses you before you agree.

'No police,' he says again. 'Or no girl.'

In the early evening you wait for him at the bypass. He is younger than his voice suggests, the brown-eyed man who pulls up in the van. You show him the pendant, and the holdall with the plastic shopping-bag inside it, stuffed with money, and he nods and reaches over, opening the passenger door. Underneath his denim jacket his T-shirt says *Just Do*

It, and the ashtray is a cairn of butts. The rear of the van is stacked with empty cages, dozens of them, smeared with droppings, and the plume from the cigarette that's wedged between his fingers cannot hide the feral stink.

You ask him about her. 'Soon,' he says, pointing out through the front windscreen at the way ahead, and your hands tighten on the holdall as the van rattles along narrow country roads, the cages clattering in the back. *Taller*, you think, *she will definitely be taller. And blonde, yes, still blonde. But that coat she'd been wearing, the one you and Donald chose for her together, her favourite, the brown fake sheepskin with the flower-embroidered sleeves, the one in all the posters; that coat probably no longer fits her.* At the outskirts of a midland town the van veers off into a housing estate. In the twilight children are playing on a green area littered with the bones of long-dead machinery, and out of habit you lean forward to look at them more closely, to see if you can recognise her. The van drives into a crescent and stops outside the furthest house. The young man points to the front door but does not follow you, and when you press the doorbell a shape comes towards you on the far side of the frosted glass, and you hear the clicking of the latch.

The woman answering the door is older than you: a hank of steel-grey hair, the creases on her face like hunting trails on an ancient map. Again you show the pendant and the holdall, and she ushers you in through the narrow hallway, past the closed door of a living room from which you can hear low voices and the sound of a television, a game-show in full swing.

You follow the woman down into the kitchen. Crusted dishes fester in the sink. The wall behind the cooker is stained with grease. On the window sill a radio is playing country and western, the rich Mississippi baritone of Charley Pride wondering 'Is Anyone Going to San Antone'. The woman pulls a chair out from the table and motions to you to sit.

'So where is she?' you ask, your voice louder than you'd intended.

The woman shakes her head, pretending not to understand.

'Here,' you say, lifting the holdall on to the table and shaking it, 'here. Look.'

'Please,' the woman says. She calls out through the doorway, and from upstairs a voice answers, in a language you do not recognise. The woman closes the door and sits down opposite you.

'We wait,' she says, and she smiles quickly at you before she looks away.

A pair of child's jeans are hanging over the back of a chair. 'Folsom Prison Blues' is playing, Johnny Cash twanging away on the guitar. The grimy window where the radio sits gives out onto a small back garden; the light is almost gone, but you can make out an upturned tricycle on an unkempt patch of grass. At the end wall there is a wooden shed, the door bolted and padlocked, with a window covered by what looks like wire mesh.

The woman is bent over her phone, its icy glow

reflected in her face. In the distance a car revs up, backfires and pulls away.

'Christine,' you say to her. No day passes without you saying it, repeating it to yourself, as if naming your loss could fill the space that's left behind, a space widening and deepening since that moment in the shopping mall when you turned around to find your daughter gone.

You rustle the contents of the holdall again, and the woman looks up.

'Her name is Christine,' you say. 'Did you know that?'

A dog is barking, somewhere among the houses in the estate; it barks and barks and barks, and then it stops.

'Chris...tine,' the woman repeats carefully, nodding. 'Yes,' she says then, returning to her phone.

Now Patsy Cline comes on, singing 'Crazy'. Half-listening, you peer again out at the shed. There is a ledge beside the window, with a little opening guarded by a grille, and you are wondering what this could be for when you see a movement, in behind the mesh.

Patsy is belting it out, her voice freighted with anguish and despair. Another flicker, and another; something is alive out there, in the shed. You stand up, pushing back your chair, and the woman's eyes widen in alarm. 'Please,' she says, making the flattening gesture with her hand: *calm down, this is under control.*

'I just... my... I just want...' you say, spluttering as you point out the window, out towards the bottom of the garden.

'No, no,' the woman says, rising to her feet. 'Please,

lady,' she says, and her hand is still outstretched when the door from the hall into the kitchen opens and a girl is standing in the doorway, with yellow hair falling over the shoulders of her coat, a fake sheepskin with flowers on the sleeves.

And Patsy's in the zone, crooning about loneliness and the blues. The woman looks at you and gestures, almost proudly, at the girl. 'Your daughter,' she says.

How often have you imagined this? How many times have you tried to will this moment of reunion into being: your daughter, running towards you, hurling herself at you as you pull her in, inhaling her, her hair, her breath, her skin? You step towards her, your arms held wide in welcome, waiting for her, your lungs gasping for air, since you are briefly unable even to speak. The girl hesitates, then scampers over to the woman and wraps herself around her, her face pressed in against the top button of the woman's jeans. The woman shrugs, a wordless half-smile at you — *children, eh?* — and bends to whisper into the girl's ear, eyeing as she does the holdall on the table. The girl turns towards you in a slow and doubtful pirouette. The woman gives her a nudge, and the girl edges across the kitchen. Tentatively she leans into you, her face gingerly touching your waist, and as you close your arms around her, immediately you know.

Now Patsy's lush contralto starts winding up for the big tear-filled finish.

You stroke her hair, feeling its brittleness, its dryness, the strands coarsened by the cheap blonde dye which is already growing out. The woman says something quickly, something you do not understand, and in response the girl slides her reluctant hands further around your waist. You bend to nuzzle her, seeing the dark roots at the crown of her head, and you try to breathe her in, although you know you will not recognise the slightly musty odour of this girl, the stale tang of her breath.

Outside a pigeon comes wheeling in over the garden, a plump grey shape hovering over the shed before it lands. It perches on the little ledge, fluttering to itself. You hear another sound then, faint at first: it is the girl, whimpering, her bony shoulders juddering under her coat. You hold on even tighter as she wriggles, struggling to get away; you hold on for dear life until the girl wrenches herself free and rushes back across the kitchen, throwing herself against the woman who admonishes her quietly, trying to soothe her, but the girl will not let go.

She sings out the final line, Patsy, holding that last 'crazy' as she wrings out every ounce of heartbreak and regret.

From the far side of the table the woman looks at you and frowns, pausing for a moment before she yanks the bulging plastic shopping bag out of the holdall.

'Now you must leave,' she says.

In the dusk the pigeon leans against the grille. Inside the shed the others jostle for position at the mesh; the grille opens, and the pigeon disappears.

'Christine,' you say, as you reach out towards her, a supplication: *please, take my hand.* The girl whines again, clings more tightly than ever to the woman's waist.

And even though you know, you keep on saying it, over

and over, like a prayer. 'Christine,' you say to this girl with the wrong forehead, and too-high cheekbones, and eyes of almost the same blue.

PROMISE

His visitors tried so hard to be cheerful. Neil could see that although they feared the worst, they painted bright smiles on their faces, telling themselves that if they were positive, he would be positive as well. Then the door of the ground-floor apartment would open; they would step inside and see for the first time the piles of cards and letters, the clutter of wires and tubes and screens, and Neil, sitting amidst all this, like a deposed king waiting for the executioner's axe to fall.

And always they recoiled when they saw the chair. Neil had flinched himself when his mother wheeled it through the hospital to take him home. The fund-raising had started while he was still in the rehabilitation wing; one of the Appeal's first purchases had been the chair. With its padded cushions and headrest, and its specially designed ventilator-unit at the back, it looked more like a dentist's chair than those worn-down threadbare versions he'd seen patrolling the wards. The leatherette covers shone and the spokes gleamed. But it was still a chair.

Why had he flinched when he'd seen it? He was leaving the hospital; he was going 'home'. It should have been an occasion for relief (if not celebration). Besides, it wasn't as if he'd thought that he would walk away unaided, away from the bedpans and the bowel evacuations, away from the curious gaze of the other patients and the breezy vigour of the nurses. The doctor had been quite clear. When a second opinion had been sought the new consultant had been clearer still. 'Not possible, I'm afraid. Not after this. Spinal cord, C 2. There's always stem cell, I suppose, but I wouldn't count on anything.'

He looked around the apartment. Angelo, the Filipino nursing assistant, had been busy with the tinsel. 'Brighten the place up for Christmas,' his mother had directed. The diminutive Angelo had set ruthlessly about this task. Ropes of gold and silver adorned pictures, door-heads and window frames; how had he managed to reach up so high? A single glittering green hawser hung over the length of the 40-inch TV screen the Appeal had also acquired. 'You'll be able to watch all the rugby on the planet,' they assured him, and it was true. With Angelo or Petr (his other nursing assistant; Czech, enormous, wordless) operating the remote, day or night there was always a match on somewhere. Despite what had happened, he'd continued to watch avidly. He'd never blamed the game. His injury was; well, unlucky. It could have happened anyone. They knew that also, the teammates and supporters who called to see him a little less often these days. Wrong place, wrong time;

it could have been any one of them.

When Ireland won the Six Nations the captain and most of the team came to visit. They presented him with a signed jersey and chatted for more than an hour. He'd known a few of the players from before, from squad sessions together; he'd played on an underage team with one of them. They crowded into the apartment; hulking, good-humoured, decent men. There was talk of more fund-raising for the Appeal, talk even of a charity CD; much laughter as to who was the worst singer. One or two of them strolled around the apartment, pausing to look at the hoists and pulleys and supports, the monitors and charts, the jars of pills. Gesturing towards the chair, they made light as best they could; jokes about car insurance, and whether Jeremy Clarkson had invited Neil to make an appearance on *Top Gear*. Each time they took the field these men put their bodies on the line in clashes so intense it hurt to watch; they did not take a step back. But here, surrounded by all the contraptions and appliances, the drugs and the devices assembled to try to hold together the pieces from the wreckage of a life, he could sense their unease, the wordless fear, flickering behind their eyes.

How empty the apartment felt when they had gone! This was the part of visits he hated, the winter silence that descended afterwards. In the bleakness of their absence he always felt lonelier than before. His mother came every day, carrying more cards and letters. He watched her slit the envelopes one after another, reading out each well-meaning message of support. *Never give up. Keep fighting. We're with you all the way.* But of course, they weren't.

He sighed. Four o'clock. Simon should be here soon. Six foot three, with a voice like a foghorn, he filled the apartment on his own. 'Now then,' he'd blare, as Angelo looked on in awe, 'what have you been up to today?' They'd met at college, at a training session. Neil was all dodge and feint; Simon was bruise and bash. Rapier, bludgeon. The next day Simon had spotted him walking across the courtyard. 'Neil!' he boomed, oblivious to the two terrified Japanese tourists nearby who had dropped instantly to their knees. Neil adored him.

They'd played together in university; Simon scrum-half, Neil out-half. In their last year the college had won promotion to Division One; Neil was top points scorer. It seemed certain they would soon both play for Ireland. Clubs from across the water had already come discreetly calling. Simon, Neil; Neil, Simon: *The Odd Couple*, one rugby correspondent had dubbed them. In team huddles before games there was a comic incongruity about the pair, Simon looming beside Neil, his arm wrapped brutishly around Neil's neck in awkward solidarity.

He could hear Angelo clattering about in the kitchen, the radio tinkling out songs of peace and joy and snow. Was Christmas that close? This time last year, his mother had asked: 'What do you want for Christmas?' He'd struggled to answer; there was nothing he could think of. Twenty-one, his postgraduate degree almost finished, the provincial management asking if he'd sign a contract, his flat in the little redbrick near the canal he shared with a couple of his teammates. And Anna; spirited, sexy, leggy. What more was there?

He listened. Outside, distant car-noise, the slish of tyres going by in the rain. The music of movement, of momentum. Since he'd come home from the hospital he'd been out on several occasions. To Mass, his mother pushing him up the side-aisle to the front where she prayed patiently for a miracle. The lads had taken him to pubs, matches, breezily assuring him that they'd make certain he did not miss out. Behind the goalposts he'd inhaled the damp air, listening to the roars of supporters, the thud and crunch of bodies colliding on the field. Afterwards in the corner of the heaving bar he would at first delight in the chatter and the clink of glasses, the giddy prancing girls, guffaws of laughter from the beery hearty men who sat beside him, taking turns. Later in the evening one or two young ones would totter over to take a look, moist-eyed with sympathy and vodka. 'You're gorgeous,' gasped one of them once, kissing him on the cheek before returning to her friends. He watched her as she left, a pair of skin-tight jeans disappearing into the maw of the crowd, the night, the life he no longer had.

Anna. They'd been together just over a year before the accident; there was no guarantee it would have lasted anyway. She'd hung on gamely for a while; tearful visits to the hospital, and later to the apartment. But the visits became shorter as she became more and more distracted by what he'd long since realised: that this was it. The pressure-sores and the spoon-feeds, the rhythmic, constant wheezing of the ventilator pumping air in through the hole in his trachea: this was all there was, all there ever would be.

He'd seen it one night on television. Switzerland. It wasn't cheap, as one might expect from a country already providing another kind of final resting place, the bank vaults like hidden tombs stacked high with hoarded millions. Obviously the Appeal could never—would never—pay. The Appeal was after all dedicated to keeping Neil alive. But Simon had organised it; the forms, the appointments with the Director of the Centre and the counsellors, and the plane tickets to Zurich (one return, the other one-way). All to coincide with the first away international match of the season, against Italy. 'Rome,' Simon had explained to Neil's mother. 'My treat. I promised. Call it a Christmas present.' There'd be no need for Angelo or Petr; he knew what to do and would be with Neil all the time. His mother hesitated initially, but later had agreed. What else could she do, with Neil insisting that this trip meant so much? 'So kind,' she'd smiled, blinking back tears. Simon had smiled back weakly; Neil too.

He couldn't have told them. Couldn't. They would have put a stop to it immediately; he knew also they would have assumed responsibility for his intentions, as they had assumed responsibility for everything else in his life. His mother would have sobbed quietly about the sacredness of human life and would have redoubled her prayers and devotions to the saints. His friends would have been stunned, bemused. He imagined them arguing with him:

did it take more bravery to die than to live? He could imagine also the hurt, the sadness in the eyes of the Appeal volunteers. He would have been begged and hectored and implored to think again. But he *had* thought about this, again and again and again. It wasn't the pain; the drugs worked, mostly. He had every gadget going. He even had enough money, for the moment. What he didn't have was a future.

Simon had refused point-blank at first. 'No way. It's illegal, anyway. No, absolutely no way; you're on your own on this one.' *Exactly*. Neil had wept then, one of the few times since he'd left the hospital, wept as he'd explained that although he'd made the decision on his own, he couldn't do it on his own. Simon had pleaded. 'Ask your mother then. Ask your sister. Not me.' But Neil had persisted. 'You're the only one I know who'll say yes, the only one I trust.' More than anything else in life he wanted this, and only Simon could deliver. His mother, his sister; out of the question. Angelo or Petr; no. Even if either had been tempted by the substantial cash offer he'd considered, they'd be…just wrong.

The facilities offered by the Centre seemed excellent. A room the size of a really good hotel room, with a table and chairs where 'those you wish to accompany you' could sit with you for a last drink. And a bed. There was a medical assistant standing by, and a counsellor who was obliged to speak with you in advance on the same day 'to make sure you were proceeding freely with your decision.' Well, 'freely'; what did that mean? But certainly it was his decision, his alone. He'd even promised Simon he'd leave a note, taking all responsibility, apologising for what would seem to some like cowardice. Absolving Simon from all blame. And Simon, exhausted after weeks of Neil nagging and cajoling, had relented. They both knew the promise of exoneration meant nothing; that always afterwards there would be fingers pointed at Simon: *You could have stopped him.* Simon would carry this burden from now on, just as he would carry Neil from the chair for the last time, carry him to the pristine-sheeted bed beside a window that gave out onto snow-covered mountains.

There had been ten minutes left to go in the game. They'd been leading by seven points; Neil was certain they'd win. A big forward had come round the back of a scrum, trundling straight at him; he'd tackled him, and they'd gone down. Others arrived on either side to join the heaving mass of limbs scrabbling for the ball. He'd fallen slightly awkwardly, but wedged in at the bottom he'd felt quite safe, waiting for the ruck to end. One of the opposition was raking him with his boot. The studs dragged across his shorts, his thigh, his socks; it hurt and would hurt more later, but he'd been here before. And then he'd heard a roar of protest from his own side, a deep sonorous voice he knew so well swearing vengeance as it thundered into the ruck. Everything changed then; the new impetus driving the opposition back, driving Neil's body forward, forward, forward—except for his head and neck which had remained pinned against the dewy grass, the cold earth. He thought he'd heard a click; the vertebrae in his neck cracking under the pressure, unable to hold his spinal cord in place. The referee had whistled immediately, a short panicky blast which meant things were bad. The last voice he heard before he blacked out was Simon's, nervous, anxious, contrite, promising him it wasn't serious. Promising that the stretcher and the straps and head brace the emergency personnel were expertly fitting into place were only a precaution. Promising Neil that, no matter what, everything would be fine.

SIX MILES EITHER SIDE

Henry's father had been late collecting him from his mother's house, and by the time they arrived at Mannion's all the good tables were gone. They stood at the reception desk while the manageress frowned and studied the seating plan. Henry was tall; at thirteen, already gaining on his father, although his shoulders had begun to slump as if carrying some burden. Eventually they were shown to a small table at the back of the mezzanine. 'Sunday brunch is finished,' the manageress said, handing them menus, 'but the special's nice. Cod.'

They ordered, and their food came quickly, chicken wings for Henry, a burger for his father. Henry's chair faced the bathrooms; his father's faced the canvas TV screen, where the game they'd come to watch was already under way. They followed the same side: the team Henry's father had supported all his life, the team that Henry had decided also to support, four years ago, when they all lived under the same roof.

'So what'ya think?' his father said. His eyes were fixed on the big screen over Henry's shoulder.

'Dunno,' said Henry, pushing away his empty plate. He contorted himself briefly to look at the action behind him. One of their team skied a good chance over the cross bar and grimaced at his teammates as he trotted back up the pitch.

'Your man Pocino's shite,' he said.

'He is,' agreed his father. 'Absolutely useless.'

Henry leaned back in his chair. He liked Mannion's, with its high ceilings and brass rails and multiple televisions. Anyway, he'd already seen everything in the cinema, and it was better than walking the pier, or hanging out in the apartment, although the apartment was off limits now that Rose was there. He glanced across the table. His father was leaning forward, studying the big screen, his hands joined over his nose in a little tent of prayer. When he'd arrived to collect Henry, his hair had been still damp from the shower; he'd smelled sweet, and clean, and Henry'd wondered if his father would one day marry Rose. He looked down at the tables thronged below them in the bar. A sadness swelled inside him, a sadness he'd felt before but could not explain.

'Ah, get up out of that, would you!' said his father, hands half-raised in exasperation as one of the opposition writhed in apparent agony on the ground. In the break of play that followed as the player was tended to, Henry's father turned towards his son.

'Why don't you come round?' he said, edging his chair

over to make room.

Henry shook his head. 'I'm ok here,' he said.

'Plenty of space,' said his father, moving his chair further; and Henry, who was not unkind, scooched his own chair over so that their knees were almost touching under the table.

'That's better,' his father said. 'Now you can see what's happening.'

He stretched his arm out across the back of Henry's chair and touched for a moment his son's shoulder. On the TV a corner kick came floating in, and was about to go harmlessly out of play when Pocino, loitering at the far post, stuck out his leg. The ball skidded off his shin and described a slow parabola past a defender's despairing lunge, bouncing between the posts before landing with a rasp against the back of the net. Men were on their feet in the bar cheering, clenched fists raised in triumph. Henry's father stood as well, his eyes glittering as he turned and tried to lift his son in a bear-hug. Henry half-stood and patted his father on the back; the two grinned at each other, and then sat down. In the slow-motion replay the looping trajectory of the ball into the net seemed comical, absurd. Pocino's teammates mobbed him, kissing with fierce delight his cheeks, his neck, his hair.

'Hullo, Henry,' a man's voice said behind them.

A dog, someone said later. Or a fox. Or maybe even a small horse. Horses had been noticed there before, grazing on the embankment beside the motorway. But if it had been a horse the boys would have seen it, or some of them would have anyway, before the bus swerved, and none of the remaining boys could remember seeing anything. 'I don't know what it was,' said Valentine, the chubby, popular bus driver, 'but there was definitely something.'

Henry looked over his shoulder at the man standing behind his chair, waiting. His father was still watching the TV screen as the goalkeeper plucked the ball out of the net and kicked it disconsolately downfield.

'Hullo, Mr Banks,' said Henry.

Henry's father turned towards Banks, an eyebrow raised: *do I know you?*

'Ian Banks,' the man said, putting out his hand. 'Bernard's Dad.'

Barnyard, they'd called him, Henry remembered: a harmless enough nickname, and he *was* harmless, small and pale and thin, with front teeth that protruded like his dad's.

'Bernard…yes, of course. Yes.' Henry's father extended his own hand. 'Harry Cox,' he said, 'Henry's Dad. I'm so sorry,' he said then, 'I really am.'

'Yes. Well. Thanks.' Banks hesitated before motioning towards the table. 'Do you mind if I…?'

Please, thought Henry, please don't let Barnyard's father sit down here.

'Of course,' said Henry's father.

Banks pulled up a chair from a nearby table and sat opposite them, his back to the big screen. 'So,' he said. He turned towards Henry and tried to smile. 'And how are you, Henry?'

Henry slid his finger inside his left sleeve and touched the scab that was halfway up his lower arm. He could not look at Barnyard's father. 'I'm fine,' he said.

'Good, good.' Now Banks turned towards Henry's father. 'Well. We went to see Phibbs again yesterday,' he said.

Henry's father nodded. Phibbs, the solicitor, was the mother of a boy two classes above Henry; like other parents, she'd attended each of the four funerals.

'The thing is,' Banks said, 'she thinks there might have been a problem with a tyre.'

Henry stared at the big screen. The opposition were pressing for an equaliser, shot after shot raining in on goal.

'Hard to say, of course,' said Banks, 'because of what happened to the bus. The fire, I mean.' He swallowed. 'But if it was a tyre...well, that's down to the bus company, isn't it?'

'I suppose,' said Henry's father, looking at the table.

'And the council as well, because of the barrier. You know about the barrier?'

Photographs were hung in the school hall of the four boys, a candle burning quietly under each one. Pictures and letters and even flowers had been taped to their lockers; they looked like shrines.

'The barrier was completely wrong!' Banks picked up a beermat and began turning it over and over against the surface of the table. 'Those motorway barriers, there are regulations. One post every six feet, it's supposed to be. And three pins on each post, to hold the barrier-rail in place. But at the bend where… at the bend, it was *twelve* feet, and then another twelve, so two posts missing. And the post that *was* there had only one pin. One pin, to hold that rail, for twenty-four feet. Phibbs says it's criminal.'

'I can see…' Henry's father glanced at his son: *are you ok?*

'And Valentine,' said Banks, 'must just have been going way too fast. I mean, it stands to reason.'

A goal, a goal at the far end, a shot from outside the box rocketing into the top corner of the net. One-all: the goal-scorer wheeled away towards the corner-flag and began a little rain dance of celebration. On the halfway line Pocino, hands on hips, was glaring at his goalkeeper.

'Phibbs says we should sue them all.' Banks was jabbing at the air with the beermat. 'The bus company, the council, Valentine, the whole lot of them. We make them…' and here he paused '…accountable.'

What he'd first noticed was a difference in the light, in how the sun came slanting through the windows after the bus had finally come to a halt, perched at an angle at the bottom of the embankment below the ruptured barrier and the motorway, curving indifferently away. He'd heard the gurgle of the exhausted engine and the drip of sweetly stinking diesel, and Valentine roaring at them, dragging as many of them as he could out of the bus, and pushing them away. He'd been one of the first out, stumbling on a concrete block that had been lying in the grass: the edge of it had grazed his left arm. He was getting to his feet, Valentine urging them to run, for God's sake, run when the hydraulics failed and the doors closed with a hiss on Barnyard and the others left inside.

Banks put the beermat down. 'It's not about the money,' he said. 'I mean, you're taking a case as well, aren't you? For Henry here?' Banks smiled weakly towards the boy.

'Well…' Henry's father looked at his shoes: it was one of the things he and Henry's mother had not yet properly discussed.

'You have to,' said Banks. 'Everyone has to. So that…' He faltered, and when he spoke again his voice sounded different, as if it was coming from some other place. 'Phibbs says the most we'll get, each of the four families, is thirty-five. The funeral expenses, they'll pay those as well. And the inquest. But otherwise, thirty-five. Thirty-five thousand euro. That's the maximum, Phibbs says. It's the law. So what do you think of that, huh?'

'It sounds…' Henry's father began to speak, thinking Banks was finished.

But Banks was not finished.

'Tell you what I think. It's an insult, that's what it is. Phibbs agrees. Thirty-five, I said to her, is that what my boy's worth? Is that what *your* boy, Henry here, is worth?'

Henry's father shook his head. Say something, Henry thought, say something so we can go, and leave this man to his grief.

'Those two missing posts,' continued Banks, 'they each

cost two euro. And the pins, the pins that should have been there, they each cost ten cents. So with their money, the thirty-five, I could buy enough posts and enough pins to... to run the barrier-rail all along the motorway for six miles either side. You see? D'you see?'

Again Henry's father shook his head, more slowly this time, before he rose reluctantly. 'We really have to leave,' he said, glancing at Henry. 'But I'm truly sorry about your son.' He stretched out his hand to Banks, who took it but did not get up.

'You know what my wife said last night?' Banks was still holding Henry's father's hand. '"One more time," she said. "I just want to see him one more time." So I said, "We'll get through this, Laureen. I know we will." But then she said, "I don't want to get through. I just want to stay here. Except I can't."' Banks looked up at Henry's father. 'You see, before this,' he said, 'we weren't always getting on that great, Laureen and I. But now we are. Now, we're even closer than before. Can you believe that, can you?'

'What would you like to do?' said his father in the car.

'I don't mind,' Henry said. He reached into his jeans pocket and pulled out an iPod and a set of headphones; the lines were coiled and twisted, and he began trying to untangle them.

'We've still time,' his father said. 'We could go see that Marvel movie again. Or there's the pier.'

'I already told you, I don't care,' said Henry. He jammed the small white polished nuts of the headphones into his ears.

'Or we could just go for a spin. Let's do that, will we?' said his father, and he gunned the engine.

They drove out through the suburbs and up into the hills. The road narrowed, trees and hedges leaning in closer until they came to a kind of summit. *Viewing Point*, the sign said, beside a rubbish bin and some picnic benches. They could see pastures and knots of woodland, and the city, shimmering below them.

'Will we see if we can get the final score?' his father said, reaching towards the dial to switch on the sports programme.

They sat in the car, the voices murmuring on the radio.

'That poor man,' Henry's father said then, and Henry could feel his father looking at him.

He jabbed the volume button of the iPod up as high as it would go and reached in under his left sleeve. The doctor had warned him not to pick at it; otherwise, she'd said, there'd be a scar. Slowly he levered his fingernail beneath the scab and waited for the small familiar stab of pain and release, a pearl of blood oozing from the wound.

KANE

I nearly missed the name. Not like me; I'm usually pretty thorough. 'You'll find yourself in there one of these days, Martin,' Audrey often says, her voice rising over the radio and assorted domestic appliances toiling in the kitchen. Some are no surprise, ancient former colleagues from the courts. Others are unexpected: *suddenly*, or *after a short illness, bravely borne*. I wouldn't be looking for anyone in particular. But sometimes one would catch my eye, the bold black print snagging on my memory. I recognise that name, I'd say to myself; I know him.

We've lost three of our Sixth Year class; one heart attack, one cancer and one drowning. There must be a good few of the staff gone as well, lay and priest; we were thirty-five years out last June, so the men (and one woman) who taught us would be nearly eighty now, or more. And I do remember seeing the names of teachers from time to time. 'Poor old Bimbo,' I'd say over breakfast, or 'Ah, Tarzan's gone,'—cue various noisy observations from Audrey. The paper wouldn't supply their nicknames of course, but as soon as I'd see the name I'd have a vision of the deceased standing in front of a blackboard, trying valiantly to teach us. I think the teachers secretly enjoyed being called "Noddy", or "Spock", or "Flea". Maybe they told themselves it meant we cared.

But the man in the Deaths Column that morning never had a nickname. We didn't even use a version of his Christian name—*Thomas (Tom)*, the paper said—which we did sometimes for other priests; his surname was so perfect, so evocative in its simple single syllable that there didn't seem to be any point. *Kane.* In a school where corporal punishment flourished, how could we improve on that?

He was a baleful presence in the playground during our breaks. Other staff would lumber around breaking up fights or trying to catch us smoking; it was comical to watch them, really. But Kane just stood in the middle of the yard, glowering, saturnine; a dark stone in the middle of a stream. There was a rumour he'd broken a boy's arm a few years earlier. We were scared shitless of him.

When there was trouble, he would glide noiselessly towards its source. One time a little First Year tyke was jeering me about another abject performance by the execrable team of which I was a member, in the Schools Cup the day before. I'd warned him already, and my back was turned when a hail of conkers hit me. I knew immediately who it was. I hated football and was no use at it, but I was fast, and I caught the little gurrier by the collar of his grey flannel shirt. 'Screw you, Delany,' I said (the school was so small everyone knew everyone) and I was about to belt him when I realised I was unable to move my arm because Kane was holding my elbow without apparent effort, and staring at me. 'Don't touch him,' he said. Reluctantly I let Delany go, though in truth I had no choice, and the boy lolloped away. Kane held my arm a moment longer and then moved on. I don't know what he said to Delany, but the next day a note was shoved into my locker; an apology, in Delany's squiggly handwriting, for showing such 'disrespect'. That was the only time I came up close and personal, as they say, to Kane. But I do remember one odd detail. If a staff member stood beside you, you could smell him: b.o. (frequently), or halitosis (also frequently) or even alcohol (less frequently, but more often than you might think). With the priests you'd never smell anything, though you might see a blob of yellow on their cassock from the boiled egg they'd had for breakfast. Generally they smelled...sexless. But as Kane leaned in to warn me in that low deliberate voice, I could smell aftershave. This wasn't, I should emphasise, some perverted attempt to make himself more appealing to the boys. Just a small vanity, I suppose; why shouldn't a man dab a splash of something smelly (Blue Stratos I think, though I really am guessing here) to make him feel good about himself? But in light of everything that happened afterwards, perhaps this detail (an "island of fact", as one of my smarter Supreme Court colleagues likes to call it) was a sign, a warning of what to expect.

What we didn't expect, however, was that Raymond Rock's father would die. Raymond was handsome in a conventional way; dark wavy hair, square-jawed, sallow-skinned. I quite liked him, though he was a bit moody at times. We played on the same useless team, Raymond and I, so we saw a lot of each other. We saw a lot of Mr Rock also, his big car filled with cigar smoke as he ferried us every other weekend to more and more remote locations in search of teams we might be able to beat. He'd bellow good-naturedly from the side-line to 'get stuck in' or some other such vague exhortation. We saw a little bit of Mrs Rock as well. Jean. Back then, when every woman in the world was trying to look like Jackie Kennedy (before she became Onassis), Jean Rock was one of the few who pulled it off. She drove us to and from the midweek games, wearing a pair of white trousers and a navy blazer, with a scarf knotted around her throat. She always seemed to be tanned, and she was the first person I saw who used sunglasses as a headband. I really fancied her.

It was a huge shock to us when Mr Rock (Charles, was it?) dropped dead. Not just because of his age, though forty-eight was awfully young, even then; it was more the idea that someone you knew, someone you'd spoken to and spent time with, could actually die. At fifteen you're so alive you feel bullet-proof, and you assume everyone else you know is the same. Except they're not. The funeral Mass was huge. The whole team sat together in our uniforms in the draughty church. A few of the school's priests were on the altar; Kane was among them. Jean Rock was in the front row, with Raymond—their only child—beside her. And—though it's easy to say it now—I was certain at one stage that I saw Kane staring at her. I could have been imagining this, of course. So many witnesses who give evidence down here in the courts convince themselves they saw something which simply could not have happened; they start with the result and work backwards, superimposing the desired outcome on their recollection of events, like one of those little tin shapes which fashion dough into a star or a heart. *Cookie Cutter Justice*, the pimply postgraduate who addressed one of our tedious Judicial Conferences called it. Whereas trying to find out what *actually* happened is what we judges are supposed to do.

However, a boy's school is a Petri dish in which rumours bloom as quickly as bacteria. Soon there were other sightings, incidents, encounters: Kane at Wednesday away matches, standing quietly beside the still-grieving Mrs Rock; Kane in the front seat of her little car at the school gate, the two of them talking long after the other cars had gone. There were stories, too, that old Charlie hadn't been as uxorious as he might have been, that he'd got a secretary pregnant who'd had to leave the bank. Maybe all of these were true, maybe none of them were; I don't know. But what happened at the Trevi Fountain seemed too outlandish to be anything but true.

Brian, my brother, was the source. A plodder, Brian; he went for the safe option of joining the family firm of solicitors rather than taking his chances at the Bar like me. Perhaps it's his dullness, his utter lack of imagination which made his account of what he saw — or said he saw — so plausible. Each year at Easter, the First Years went on a trip to Rome; a chance to brush up on their Latin and to witness the glory of the seat of the One True Faith in all its majesty. One afternoon, after the boys had finished in the Keats House, Noddy and Spock, the two teachers accompanying them on the trip, had given them an hour to look around, with strict instructions to assemble by the Trevi Fountain at 4pm. Brian, typically, arrived at the appointed rendezvous ten minutes ahead of schedule, alone; he didn't even have the imagination to get lost. He was standing at the fountain, a slightly overweight, bespectacled boy perspiring in the heat when he became aware of voices beside him. Of course, there are so many different voices in the hordes that gather at the fountain that I was sceptical Brian could have recognised them. But Brian said the voices were Irish, which made him look up, and when he did he realised the voices belonged to Kane and Mrs Rock. Brian was quite certain it was them, though I don't know how well he could have known what Jean Rock looked like. But the man in the linen suit and white shirt and dark tie was, he insisted, definitely Kane. Almost without realising it, Brian opened his mouth to extend to them the courtesy, the *politesse* the school had worked so hard to instil in all of us. 'Hullo, Father,' he said. I don't think Brian would have said this in a sarcastic way; he was just too dull to have seen the rich comic opportunities of such an occasion. Kane looked up sharply, and glanced over at Brian. Then the woman — definitely Jean Rock, Brian said — tugged Kane's arm, and the pair of them drifted away into the crowd.

You have to understand it would have been impossible to suppress a story as sensational as this. Naturally, Brian told his own pathetic little band of cronies; it gave him, briefly, a currency among the more sophisticated boys in his class who otherwise would not have been seen dead in his company. Equally naturally, he told me, his older brother. Brian knew Raymond; he'd met him in our house, and as I say the school was so small, so intimate that everyone knew everyone else anyway. So anybody could have written what appeared on the blackboard that morning a few weeks later, during the summer term, since it is reasonable to assume that by then *everybody* knew; though of course I'd never mentioned it to Raymond, who could hardly have missed the sniggering, the whispers among little knots of boys when he was near. In which case the scurrilous message chalked up when we trooped in that morning for first class (Geography, Flea) was simply a crude articulation of something Raymond must have been aware of all along. Or else he hadn't known at all.

'Seats, boys, seats,' said Flea as he bounded into the classroom. Everyone scrambled to their desks. Flea hadn't yet noticed the message scrawled near the bottom left hand corner of the blackboard, like a sly footnote; I'm pretty sure Raymond didn't see it either until he was sitting down. No one spoke but there were nudges and giggles as the boys at the front read it; soon the dullards at the back were half-standing in their seats, trying to make out what it said. The last person to see it was Flea. He glanced at it initially and then did a double-take, peering at the words before turning back grimly to the smirking class. 'Who wrote this?' he said.

At this remove it's easy to acknowledge that the words used were a shameful, vile allegation against any boy's mother. And yet there was a wittiness, a cleverality in the rhyme scheme that could not but have appealed to our brute sensibilities as fifteen-year old boys: the way the *Rock* in the first two words *Mrs* and *Rock* chimed with the last two words, *Kane's* and *cock*, with the whole poem, the whole line hinging on the middle of the five words, *sucks*. I remember looking at Raymond; I was sitting alongside him. His cheeks were suffused with red and he was breathing more and more quickly. No one answered Flea's question. Flea waited a moment and asked again, but still there was no response. 'Disgraceful,' said Flea, shaking his head. He glanced at Raymond before he turned to the blackboard and briskly scrubbed away the words with a duster. A murmur of excitement swelled in the room while Flea's back was turned, but there was another noise also, a wretched wailing as Raymond, his head bowed, began to weep. His chest heaved as he attempted to draw breath; he drew his hands up to his face to try to stem the stew of tears and mucus and saliva which was already dripping on his desk. For a moment the room was silent except for the sound of Raymond's sobs. Flea quickly produced a wrinkled handkerchief and escorted the stricken boy to the bathroom; when he returned, alone, there was a whiteness to his fury we'd never seen before. 'You bastards,' he said, bouncing up and down in his little rubber shoes. I think we were genuinely taken aback by his anger: when he asked a third time who'd written the words in question he was shouting, though again nobody answered. He ordered the class to write out the first ten pages of our Geography textbook. There were some half-hearted grumbles of 'That's not fair, Sir,' but Flea flung the door open, announced he was going for the headmaster, and warned us to be quiet; and even though there were one or two sniggers at first, eventually the only noise was the scratching of nibs moving quickly across paper as the air thickened with the sense that something had been breached.

Raymond's desk was empty for the few remaining weeks of term, and after the summer there was a new boy in his place. We heard later he'd gone to an even smaller school further out of town. He never attended any of our school reunions, though his name sometimes came up towards the end of those garrulous evenings when we'd gather drunkenly around a table and try to reconstruct our schoolboy lives. (He's an estate agent, someone said.) I did see him once, about four years ago. Audrey and I were waiting for our bags at the airport when I realised that he was standing at the next carousel. I saluted him warily, so that I could pretend it was an accident if he ignored me, which he did. 'Who was that?' asked Audrey as we wheeled our trolley towards the exit. 'Oh, just someone I thought I recognised,' I said. I have no doubt that he saw me, and knew exactly who I was.

Kane never returned. A terse note accompanying our summer reports indicated Fr Kane had retired from the teaching staff and the community of the school. One boy in our class—Darcy, I think—had it that he'd been sent out to the missions. I know now that some orders would quietly ship out their turbulent priests. But Kane wasn't a priest, not by then. *Deeply regretted by his wife Jean,* the death notice said. Kane's visit to Rome, we discovered later, had been for his laicisation, for which he had to apply to the Holy Father in person. Fitzgerald — who eventually became a Third Secretary in Foreign Affairs — said he saw him many years later, at the far end of a corridor in a museum in Venice, Jean Rock by his side, but by the time he'd ambled up to greet them, they were gone.

Greatly missed by Raymond. Was Rock my friend? I suppose so, though he was not a close or intimate companion. Insofar as I spent time with him dawdling between classes, or playing cards at lunch break, or plodding in the rain around the rugby pitches that are now apartments, then, yes, Raymond was my friend. I wrote those words on the blackboard that summer morning not because I no longer liked Raymond, but because I loved Jean Rock. I loved her, and now she had been taken from me by a man who'd promised God he'd never touch a woman; and, because he'd broken that promise so that he could be with her, she would never leave him. I know it sounds risible; a fifteen-year old in love with a woman almost three times his age. But what is love anyway? Not those pigtailed giggly sisters of our classmates, or the poised elegance of the girls attending the nearby convent-school; that wasn't love, no more than Audrey, decent old hatchet that she is, is love now. I'll tell you what love is. One Wednesday afternoon, long before all this, we were coming back in Rock's car from a match. Raymond was in the front, and Darcy and Fitzgerald and me were in the back, still in our football gear, muddy and elated; we'd won, a rare victory, against a smaller and even more unfashionable school. I was sitting in the middle, only half-conscious of the suburbs flashing by: I was studying Jean Rock, her bronzed and jewelled hands calmly holding the steering wheel, the elegant sweep of her jaw, the way her lustrous auburn hair fell to exactly the right place on her shoulders. 'The best day ever,' Darcy was screeching, with Fitzgerald grunting his approval and Raymond murmuring assent. 'Oh boys,' said Jean Rock smoothly, 'I'm sure there are even better days ahead for all of you. Isn't that right, Martin?' She smiled at me in the rear-view mirror; I looked away and then immediately looked back. 'Oh *yeah*, Mrs Rock,' I said, and the way it came out, everyone in the car laughed. 'You're a scream, Martin,' said Jean as she returned to look at the road in front of us. I leaned my head against the headrest and eyed the rear-view mirror, in case she might glance back at me again.

RAINBOW BABY

Lesley wants to know how I'm getting on with Joey. 'How would you assess your relationship?' she says to me, flicking through the file that's open on her desk. I'm in Lesley's office; there are files everywhere, stacked up on shelves and chairs and all around the floor, like wobbly manila tower blocks. 'On a scale of one to ten?' she says. Lesley is the psychiatrist here at The Farm, so she's allowed to ask. She looks at me over her glasses. The middle bit is broken, held together by Elastoplast. *Two,* I want to say. Which might even be an overstatement. Because although I did what I did for both of us, Joey still doesn't understand, and doesn't want to talk about it. 'You just need to get well, Mar,' he says each time he visits, and when I try explaining he sighs and folds his arms. I look across the desk at Lesley. 'Seven and a half?' I say. Lesley makes a squiggle with her biro.

The Farm had been my barrister's idea. 'Just a couple

of weeks,' he said, though it turned out to be six. 'They'll do an assessment which we can hand in to court. It's bound to be of help.' He was wearing a big black boot on account of a skiing injury. 'Because nobody,' he said, '*nobody* would have done what you did, Marian, unless they were…you know, fragile.' When the barrister said this Joey nodded sadly, although he wouldn't look at me. What happens when you stop liking the one you love? Because he did love me before this, and he'd wanted one just as much as I did, maybe even more. When we went to see the consultant after the first time, Joey'd been the one who'd started crying first. She wore bright red lipstick, the consultant, and her mouth glistened as she nudged the box of tissues towards us, explaining that this *happens*, even to healthy couples.

'And family?' says Lesley. That word: *let's start, let's have.* I close my eyes. 'Your *own* family, I mean,' Lesley says, a hand half-raised in apology. 'Father, mother?' Dad is five years gone this year; heart-attack on the fourth green. I wish he'd met Joey. My mother still plays, sprightly in her slacks and sweater, scent of sauvignon; *The Merry Widow*, they call her in the golf club. And so competitive. She did ask one Sunday when she came to dinner if there was 'a problem'. 'We're in no hurry,' I said, trying to smile as I rammed the dishes into the dishwasher. 'What's meant for you won't pass you by,' she said then, though I could see her eyeing Joey up and down when he came back into the kitchen. My one brother lives in Australia. No sisters. Joey, though, has three of them, all proud mothers of red-cheeked sugar junkies tearing in and out of rooms and bawling their eyes out while the husbands ladle out spaghetti hoops. The three of them take turns inspecting me for signs of progress, frowning at my flat belly, my brimming wine glass. 'Is there a friend that you'd be close to?' Lesley says, making another squiggle. 'Well,' I say, 'there's Eva.' Twenty Camels daily, diamanté nose-stud and a tattoo of barbed wire around her ankle. 'You'll need to pack these in if you're serious about a sprog, Mar,' she'd said as we shivered in the car park of St Damien's where we taught, the wet tarmac carpeted with cigarette butts. 'I know,' I'd said, tossing the fag-end away after one last salt-sweet drag as the school bell clanged over the tannoy, demanding our return. 'There,' I'd said, 'I'm ready.' And I was. The second time, after Joey and I'd come back from holidays in Malaga and Joey'd started calling it 'José' although we didn't even know yet if it was a boy or a girl, I'd wanted to tell Eva. But Joey wouldn't let me. So we didn't tell anyone. Which, as it turns out, was just as well.

Where the hospital is now there used to be an actual farm, with pigs and hens and fields of wheat. They sold off the rest of the land years ago for houses, but you can still see where the barn was, and the yard, though now it's flower-beds and polytunnels. There's an older man who's here every day, planting. I see him as I walk the paths among the petalled borders. Another client; they don't say 'patient' in here. I tell him how lovely the flowers are, and he smiles at me in slow motion; maybe it's the medication. 'Marigolds,' he says. He looks away then, his gloved fingers burrowing into the earth. I stand a moment longer, admiring the reds and oranges and yellows, their beautiful delicate heads coming into bloom. In the evenings we watch TV in the common room; quiz shows and talent contests, mostly. What I like, I've discovered, are the nature programmes. The sunfish produces 300 million eggs at a time, did you know that? A baby alligator is called a hatchling. And the heart of a blue whale is the size of a car. Imagine the sound it must make, pumping all that blood around that enormous body—boom, boom, boom! And the silence when it stops.

This last time, you see, I'd been certain. As soon as I saw those two blue lines: *this is it*, I thought, *this is the one*. I could feel the weightless fullness of it inside me almost immediately, my body thickening, hips getting wider, my breasts becoming tender. No morning sickness, but a sudden ravenous desire for toothpaste. I even thought I felt it moving once; a flutter, a whispered rumour, though the consultant said this was impossible so early on. 'You'd want to put its name down for St Damien's,' said Eva, giggling as we clinked glasses. 'What I want,' I said, as I sipped my sparkling water and pointed at my navel, 'is for this to go full term.' To be one of them, those mothers parading their bumps up and down the supermarket aisles. To walk past a playground and not feel an empty swing inside me, creaking back and forth. To have someone on the bus smile and stand up and offer me their seat. I wanted to be able to pause and catch my breath, and then breathe in again the wondrous strangeness of it, happening to me. To me and Joey, the two of us. The *three* of us. I wanted the shape of it growing within me, and the others in the staffroom crowding round and asking 'when', and the daydreams about bedroom colours, and the random chatter about names, even though Joey said that this time he didn't want to jinx it, and I wanted, really *did* want, the bone-deep tiredness of it, sinking me to the bottom of the sea, my eyes closing until I'd wake to find the ultrasound technician twinkling at me as she manoeuvred the transducer over the globe of our new world, pointing at the screen, saying, 'There it is, there. Look.' But the technician shook her head. 'I'm sorry,' she said. 'I'm really, really sorry.'

'This is a profoundly distressing matter,' the judge says slowly. White-haired, crumple-faced: *you must have grandchildren by now*, I think, watching her, *do you dandle beaming tots upon your knee?* 'Distressing for *all* concerned,' she says, looking behind me at where Joey's sitting, with Eva on one side of him and The Merry Widow on the other, each holding his hand. Because there's a baby-shaped hole in Joey's life as well, isn't there? My barrister glances back at me, a hopeful eyebrow raised. The judge twitches a half-smile at Joey, and then scowls at me. 'I cannot, however, allow the seriousness of this offence to go unpunished,' she says.

This time my barrister makes a face, and I realise I'm shaking. 'Having regard therefore to the early guilty plea, the helpful psychiatric report of Dr Lesley Doran, the previous good record of the accused and the low risk of re-offending, the appropriate sentence is one of eighteen months...' A sob behind me; it's Joey, his face bowed in his hands. Eva pats him on the back as my mother fumbles for a tissue. The only other sound is the scratching of reporters' pens. But how can no one hear the air being sucked out of my body? The judge pauses, one eye on the press gallery, and continues, '...which, in the circumstances, I will suspend on a number of strict conditions...' And as she's listing off stipulations about treatment programmes and my continuing attendance at The Farm, though only as a day-patient, I look across the courtroom to where the girl is sitting. She's in a tracksuit, sandwiched between a police officer and a social worker. Scrawny, pale; she could be one of the First Years in St Damien's, though the prosecution said she'd been sixteen when it happened. She doesn't seem triumphant, or disappointed; she just seems stunned. And as I look at her, because this is the first time I've seen her since I saw her at the shopping centre, I wonder: who's minding the baby? Who's looking after him today? It was a boy, definitely. *Wayne.* Not the name I'd have chosen, but still. The girl had been standing just inside the entrance to one of the department stores, with her friend, a couple of young lads there as well, all skitting about something she was showing them on a mobile phone. I mean, what was she thinking, leaving the pram out there in the mall? I walked over and leaned in under the hood. He was asleep; I could smell Sudocreme and talcum powder and that sweet new-baby smell. *You're so perfect*, I thought as I lifted him out of the pram. Very gently; I didn't want to wake him. He was wearing a multi-coloured sleepsuit. 'Like a little rainbow, you are,' I murmured, nuzzling his downy head. Then I tucked him under my coat and started walking down the concourse.

I could hear her shouting when she came out of the department store and saw the empty pram: 'Wayne!' she said. 'Where's Wayne?' I kept walking, though the security guard outside Tesco's turned to look at me, and the bundle I had swaddled in the crook of my arm. As I passed through the revolving doors and out into the car park, I felt him stir, and start to wriggle. The girl was wailing now, her anguish piercing the air: 'My baby! Where's my baby?' I glanced inside my coat to make sure he was alright, and as I did he opened his eyes. They were the most exquisite blue. And then — maybe because he recognised his mother's voice — he started to cry. 'Shush, shush now,' I said, rocking him to try to get him back to sleep. Then I put my little finger to his lips, and immediately he stopped. For a few moments, anyway. 'That's it,' I said, soothing him as he tried furiously to suckle. Because I'd seen other mothers doing this, so I knew it was the right thing to do. The security guard had come out through the revolving doors, and was standing in the car park, looking round. But I kept going, past the exit barrier and out onto the street. I was thinking of the two of us, you see. The *three* of us, and all the things that we were going to do together.

ICHTHYANTHROPE

The easy thing would be to plead guilty. That way, they'd all get what they want. The crowd jostling outside the courthouse, hurling insults at the prison van. The journalists, tiptoeing through the legal minefield of contempt of court (my trial is still a few days off), struggling to conceal their own contempt for what I've 'done'. In one sense I can't blame them. It's what they've been brought up on, a diet of risible police procedurals consumed on sale-item couches, secure in the knowledge that the forces of law and order will triumph. *'S'alright, guvnor; it's a fair cop. You got me bang to rights, I'll come quietly.* Good always wins out over evil; isn't that what we were all taught?

But it doesn't work like that. Although you know this already, Denise, don't you? A senior counsel of your experience; you don't need me to tell you.

Is that a new shade of blue swerving over your

eyelids, by the way? The blusher on your cheeks seems pinker also; am I right? Something's different, anyway. You've changed.

'Right, Morris,' says McCutcheon, the warder; beer-bellied, a shock of prematurely white hair. 'I'll be back at five.' How touching, this use of my first name by the staff here at Ravenstone to make me feel less alienated, less vulnerable. Did you know the suicide rate among prisoners on remand awaiting trial is much higher than among prisoners serving a sentence? I'm sure you do, Denise. The prison authorities needn't worry, though; I'm not going to end it all. Why should I? I've done nothing wrong.

The door of the interview room clangs shut. Collins, the solicitor, is silent, his pen hovering above his notebook.

'Good afternoon, Mr Hooke,' you say.

Oh please now, Denise. Or should I say 'Ms English' — or *Mrs*, given the wedding band encircling your delicate ring finger. Is English your married or your maiden name, I wonder? Such a wonderful anachronism, the maiden name, replete with hints of bygone chivalry and courtly conduct as well as less gallant, darker acts. But even back then there were occasions when certain formalities could be dispensed with.

'Hello, Denise,' I say.

A tiny hesitation; you glance at Collins before you tap the doorstep of bound papers on the desk in front of you. 'Well, the prosecution has finally completed its disclosure, Mr Hooke,' you say—and I smile, interrupting you as politely as I can: '*Morris*. Please.'

Beat. 'Alright. Morris.' There is a note of discord in your voice; you cannot quite conceal your discomfort. But these are our names, Denise; these are who we are.

'So now,' you say, 'it's over to you.'

*

'Backstory'. Isn't that what the writers call it? I remember Alice talking about it. She created—she *imagined*—the most amazingly detailed lives, not just for her main characters, but for every single person in each book, even if they'd only a small walk-on part. She had a separate index card for each of them; she wrote down all the details and then stuck the cards on the wall beside her desk. 'Why on earth,' I'd ask, 'do you need to know what the groomsman who brings the king his horse is wearing?' She'd turn on me then, all snippy: 'Because,' she'd say, 'I have to be able to see these people, to hear and smell them. To feel what it's like to be in their presence, to *be* them. I have to *know* them; if I don't know them, no one else will want to know them either. Now please, Morris, go back to your antiques and leave the book-writing to me.' She had quite a sharp tongue on her at times, had Alice: combative, cynical, sarcastic. Everyone has this picture of a diminutive, jolly woman who wrote those wonderful historical novels, but that's not the *full* picture. So don't be fooled. And no, I am not trying to justify what happened. (Her death, you want me to say. But I won't. Because to me, she isn't. Dead, I mean.)

And that's what *you* want as well, Denise, isn't it? You want those little life-details that will make me a living breathing person. If you can assemble those details and present them in the right way, the hope is that the jury will see me for what I am: an ordinary man to whom something extraordinary happened (although it happened to her, not to me). Rather than the ultimate cartoon villain: a man who killed his wife.

Or is it something else you're looking for? An explanation, perhaps? Some bauble for the jury; a delusional psychosis brought on by delayed reaction to a childhood trauma, maybe, or a faithless wife? I wish I could oblige. But my upbringing was undistinguished in its cossetted bourgeois complacency. I was the only son — the only child — of Pater, a mousey career diplomat, and Mater, his shrewish wife. In fairness both of them lavished affection on me from the day I was born. Pater's postings abroad meant I attended a small private boarding school — but there is nothing for you there either. I was not happy in St Thomas's, but I was not unhappy either, and I do remember with a degree of almost fondness its tree-lined avenue, its fetid dorms and its execrable food. I had the usual schoolboy crushes on one or two of the older boys, but nothing untoward. There was no question of 'abuse'. I was being groomed for polite society; and how much more polite than an antiques dealer can one be? As for Alice, we were at all times content together, perhaps unfashionably so; the unfaithful one—albeit briefly—was not her, but me. I see in this regard that the updated disclosure documentation includes an interview with Ms Sharpe. My compliments to the redoubtable Detective Sergeant Willis for tracking her down. No, Denise—and I hope it is in order to address you by your Christian (another anachronism!) name—what is truly remarkable is not what happened to me, but what happened to Alice.

I smile. 'I think you already know,' I say, nodding at the volumes of paperwork on your side of the desk. 'It's all in there, isn't it?'

A silence. Collins fidgets in his chair.

'Maybe you should take me through it again,' you say, eyeing me steadily. A challenge: do you think I will not remember what I have already said, or do you think I will remember it too well? Very good, then; I accept.

'Of course,' I answer, 'and may I say how particularly elegant you look today.'

Oh, but you are not easily deflected. 'I think we need to focus on...'

'...That suit; is it new?'

The slightest pause before you respond. 'Eh...yes. Yes, it is. Now, can we...'

'...I thought so. Very nice indeed.'

Collins smirks a faint *well done, sir,* but I ignore him, admiring instead the well-cut lines, the discreet stitching, the darkest of silk. I try to catch your eye, but this time you look away: does flattery make you uneasy, I wonder?

'So,' I say, 'where would you like me to begin?'

*

The shop was Pater's idea. I had tried university (my school leaving results were such that I was fit for no more than a basic Arts degree) and while I enjoyed the loucheness of it, the lazy days and nights of drinking and carousing, I could not abide the lectures, the tutorials, the unrelenting ambition. One of Pater's cronies ran Perrot & Perrot, a small dusty antiques shop in a run-down corner of the city; Pater had a quiet word, and the next thing I was in. There was a shabby gentility about the place, with the usual trickle of customers; the innocents abroad, the bumptious know-it-all 'collectors', and the wily dealers looking for an unidentified masterpiece. Two years after I began working there Pater died, and Mater followed suit not long after. I inherited their small but reasonably well-located semi-d, and a modest sum of money. Pater's solicitor read the will at the mahogany boardroom table (imitation Victorian) in his office before fixing me with a rheumy eye over his rimless glasses. 'Well, Morris,' he said, 'you're on your own now.' And I was—until Alice.

I knew who she was immediately. My university career (if that's the word) may have ended with a whimper, but I remained a voracious reader, and I had devoured her three novels on the Tudor cycle. When the bell above the door sounded its prim tinkle I glanced up, not wishing to appear too desperate for custom; and there she was, alone, a smaller, greyer version of the author-photograph gracing the back of her novels. I affected not to recognise her. She patted various pieces of furniture; a chest of drawers, a chair, a coat-stand, and then ambled over to the Edwardian inlaid desk where I was sitting, doing some paperwork. 'Hello,' she said, smiling, 'I am wondering if by any chance you have any eighteenth century silver?'

Married: the sniffy description in my line of business for a piece of furniture made up of parts from two different styles or eras. We were perhaps an unlikely looking husband and wife; I am tall, with an apologetic stoop, whereas Alice was short and dumpy. Her scribbler friends wondered where I'd come from. 'This is Morris,' she'd giggle. 'I picked him up in an antique shop.' They scrutinised me with a certain steely intensity; they were polite, but only up to a point. I know that before our wedding a couple of them counselled her against me.

I have no doubt she loved me. That coven of writers will assure you she married me out of despair; and Alice did tell me that before we met, she thought she'd missed the boat. But neither of us had had 'significant others' in the past; we had both come late to the dating game, and her previous sexual experiences were as comically inept as mine. And, yes, before you ask, I *did* love her. I know how this looks; the Georgian mansion in the city centre I could never have afforded, and the cottage in Kinroan I'd persuaded her to buy. But I delighted in her perky, inquisitive demeanour, her at-times childlike innocence; and there was, in our occasional awkward fumblings between the sheets after lights out a kind of tenderness. If we were perhaps more like brother and sister: so what? Who decides, Denise, on what makes a 'good' marriage? Not the jury, anyway.

*

The pages of your brief are marked and underlined and badged with Post-It stickers. You have been busy, Denise, probing, searching for inconsistencies, inaccuracies, holes. No doubt the prosecution counsel has done the same. White-haired, ruddy-faced; Hagan, I think his name is. Yes, Hagan. I understand that your job is not to believe me, but to 'take instructions' from me and present my case in accordance with those instructions. The truth, for the purposes of the trial — *our* trial, since we are both in this together, are we not? — is what I tell you it is, not what you believe.

But I *want* you to believe, Denise; I want you to accept that what I'm telling you is the truth. Collins, head down, scribbling away; well, for him the prestige of acting for Morris Hooke, the man accused of murdering his wife the author Alice Hooke is intoxicating, but he will never be convinced of my innocence. You know that at an earlier consultation — before I met you, Denise — Collins tried to persuade me to plead guilty? A willingness to spare Alice's family the ordeal of a trial, an early demonstration of remorse; both of these, he told me, would improve my eligibility for parole. Willis had muttered something similar in the police station. Let me be clear: I have no wish to be a source of grief to Alice's family, such as it is (two cousins living in Australia, since Alice was like me an only child, her parents long since dead). Nor do I wish to enrage her legion of fans which seems to have macabrely grown in number as sales of her novels ratchet up since her death. As for remorse—well, remorse for what? I know that, in the best traditions of your profession—and to protect yourself from what might otherwise be ethically inconvenient—you will never ask me did I 'do it'. But let me reassure you anyway: I didn't.

Maybe, though, the real reason why a guilty plea would be so welcome in this case is that it would relieve you all—Willis, Collins; even you, Denise—of having to consider the alternative. Even a guilty verdict—which is almost certainly the outcome, I fully understand—will not have the same impact. There will always be that snagged loose thread, that nagging doubt (though not a 'reasonable' doubt; I know, I know)—what if the jury got it wrong? Whereas a plea of guilty means: you can relax. Forget the explanation, the story he told you; he invented it, the whole thing. He *killed* her.

Except I didn't.

You glance at Collins and then back at me. Brown eyes, high cheek-bones, dark hair cut in a bob; you are *soignée*, no doubt about it. ('Get your one Denise as your brief,' a scrawny baby-faced bank-robber advised me in here one morning as we were lining up for food. 'She's deadly. And she's a ride.') But even you enhance, embellish: a touch of eyeliner, a finger-tip of rouge, a hint of hair-colourant to add lustre. Are any of us really who we say we are, Denise; do any of us tell the truth, the whole truth and nothing but the truth?

'Perhaps,' you say, 'you could tell us a bit about the cottage at Kinroan?'

*

Vista Mare. Not our choice; the previous owners had given it the depressingly pretentious name. I'd wanted to change it, but Alice said it was bad luck, so we settled for removing the revolting terra cotta nameplate on the gate. It did have wonderful views out over the pier, Kinroan strand and the bay. 'Arcadia,' Alice said as we looked out the window at the restless sea, the estate agent lingering discreetly in the hall, 'this will be our Arcadia.' I had some notion that 'arcadia' referred to a pastoral woodland scene, but Alice preferred the more romantic association; a lost world of idyllic bliss. *Et in Arcadia ego.* And where is Alice now?

I should explain as well that I was the swimmer. I was not particularly good at it, but even as a child on holiday in the West of Ireland I had loved standing waist-high in the light green water, arms crossed beatifically over my chest. There was something glorious about submerging myself beneath the surface, the tang and gleam of it, the bracing chill; and further out the sound of it, the ocean's organ interludes. I loved as well the way the world I lived in became, briefly, the other world, muffled and distant. Here, underwater, was the *real* world, the only world that mattered. Whenever we stayed in the cottage I would make it my business to amble down each day to the beach and dive into the modest waves. Alice would come with me, although she did not swim. She *could* swim, but she chose not to; she told me once that she never really enjoyed it. She was happy to stroll along the shallows in her bare feet past fretting mothers and over-exuberant fathers indulging their shrieking young, while I would power along further out in a laboured version of what I understand is known as the American Crawl.

On the Monday after Easter, the last day of what was to be our last holiday together, we had gone as usual to the strand. It was late afternoon. The water was still icy, but there was a brightness in the air, an almost-warmth that signalled change, a new season. I lowered myself in gingerly — it really *was* cold — and began to swim. Alice walked along the beach; a couple of others were doing the same. I had completed some fifty strokes and was turning to wave to her in triumph when I saw that she had stopped and was bent double, clutching her right foot. As I swam in towards her I could hear her whimpering in pain, and I wondered had she been stung by a jellyfish. But even before I emerged from the water there was a man by her side, offering assistance; a doctor, it transpired, who quickly and confidently concluded that

Alice had stepped on a shell which had shattered. This diagnosis made perfect sense, as did the advice he gave. 'There may be something still in there,' he said, as he knelt benevolently at Alice's feet and prised the jagged fragments from her skin. 'A warm bath, that's what she needs. Opens up the pores.'

Again, let me clear; I do not blame the doctor. How could he—how could anyone—have known what would happen next?

*

You produce a pair of glasses from a leather sleeve. This section of your papers is dog-eared, well-thumbed; a photocopy of my account of events. Collins has not even bothered to have it typed up; I hope you can read my writing.

You scan the statement until you find what you are looking for, your finger landing, resting on the word.

'The bathroom, Mr—sorry, Morris.' Eyebrows furrowed, though your voice is steady.

Slowly you remove your glasses and then look at me, a theatrical flourish beloved by so many of your kind.

'Can you just explain again?' you say.

I look down. You think I'm avoiding your gaze, but I'm not.

'Yes,' I say.

Can you hear it, Denise; that semi-tone of sadness in my voice?

'Yes, I can.'

*

I went up to the house for the car and drove down to collect her. She was still wincing as she manoeuvred herself into the passenger seat. When we got back to the cottage I suggested she might try a bath, but she insisted on going straight to bed, where she slept for a number of hours. When she woke, she was a little better, though still sore, and she seemed somewhat distracted. I made supper, and afterwards we sat in the living room, watching as the darkness came rolling in across the bay.

About ten o'clock I stood up.

'Yes, yes,' she said, although I hadn't asked her anything.

'You sure you're alright?' I wondered aloud.

Alice didn't answer.

'I'm going to bed,' I said. 'Are you sure—'

She looked up. 'Actually,' she said, 'I think I'll have a bath.'

You need to understand that Alice had always enjoyed the pleasures of a languorous soak, even late at night. She'd told one journalist this was where she formulated the plots for her novels, lying back in warm water surrounded by candles, a radio playing classical music in the background. It was not unusual for her to be in there for an hour, or more. And at least she was— belatedly—following the good doctor's instructions. She limped into the bathroom, shooed me away and closed the door. So far, so normal.

'And you're certain that at that time you didn't see —' Collins interrupts, unable to contain his scepticism.

'No, Mr. Collins. I did not see the knife.'

I woke suddenly; the other side of the bed was empty. The clock said 4.10 am; even by her standards this was an unusually long immersion. I called her name, and got no reply; but I did hear something else, coming from the bathroom: the sound of splashing, vigorous and sustained. She's had a stroke, I thought at first. I ran out and knocked on the bathroom door, which as usual was locked. 'You alright?' I said. There was no reply, but the splashing stopped briefly, and then started up again. I hammered on the door. 'Swimming lessons?' I said, attempting humour, though I was obviously worried. No answer: I could only hear the faint sweet strains of Schubert from the transistor. I pressed my head against the frosted pane. The churning and the thrashing recommenced, longer this time, and so loud I could not hear the radio. 'Alice!' I said. Then I put my shoulder to the door and shoved my way in.

She was completely submerged, kicking violently, arms by her side. There were pools of water everywhere. I reached in to haul her out but as I did so she cried 'No!' and slipped my grasp, closing her eyes to plunge once more, head down, her legs scissoring all the time. 'What are you doing?' I said. Alright, shouted: I was scared, you understand. I kept trying to pull her to the surface but she was determined to stay under; it took all my strength but eventually I managed to drag her up, more brusquely this time. She gave a little gasp and slumped, her eyes still closed, into my arms.

I appreciate that what you — what the jury — need in order even to consider believing what I am saying is evidence of the kind of transformation those senti-mental Hollywood fantasies have conditioned you to expect. Skin turning to scales, the slow webbing of hands and feet, an outline of a fin emerging from the lumbar spine, that sort of thing. Did you really think, though, that a process such as this is bloodless? That the kind of metamorphosis which I'm describing could occur without the rending of flesh, without pain? Of course not.

So. The knife lay across the soap dish. Yes, Collins, the one pictured in the booklet; a breadknife, perhaps eighteen inches long, the photo of it on a table taken later in the police station laden with inferences of violence. The bath water's alarming rosy hue did make me think at first that she had tried to kill herself, but her wrists were intact. The blade's serrated edges had done their work elsewhere: there were three gashes, each about two inches long, on either side of her ribcage. I cradled her across my lap, and as I did so, she twitched and began to try to speak. She seemed out of breath, and at first I could not make out what she was saying, her voice was so weak. 'What is it?' I said. There were tears in my eyes: I admit I was weeping primarily for myself. I didn't know what was happening; I just knew I couldn't fix it. But I was weeping also for the woman in my arms, the woman I loved, (despite the prosecution's theory following the discovery of my dalliance with Ms Sharpe). I leaned in to try to hear what she was saying, and as I did so she opened her eyes, their greying blue a mirror image of the word she was whispering, over and over: 'Sea'.

*

The interview room is quiet. I can hear a gurgle somewhere in Ravenstone's late Victorian plumbing. Collins glances at his watch, wondering how much more of this he has to take. You are uncomfortable as well, Denise; your twenty years of ring-craft as an advocate have taught you to maintain a cool exterior in the face of even the most outlandish explanations offered by a client, but you are struggling with this. You fold your arms and sit back in your chair, still looking at me, and you do not say a word. I know what you are doing. You are contriving this silence to make it clear that you do not believe me. To make me feel uneasy. You think I will start babbling, unable to resist the urge to fill the vacuum you've so cleverly created.

Well, I won't.

A beat. Collins cannot bear the tension. 'But why wouldn't you just bring her to hospital?' he says, eyes narrowing to slits of contempt. You glance at him and then you raise a carefully-plucked eyebrow in my direction.

'Because I knew what she wanted,' I say.

Your arms are still folded. I can see the gleam of your wedding ring.

'Oh come on, Mr Hooke, please!' Collins throws his pen down on his legal notepad.

You raise your hand to silence him. 'Tell me,' you say, 'about Ms Sharpe.'

Ah yes, Joanna. The prosecution's trump card. I can see Hagan, his eyes roving back and forth over the faces of the jury, warming to his task: 'You will also hear, ladies and gentlemen, that the accused had been involved with a woman named Joanna Sharpe, and had promised her that he would leave his wife.' The jury will turn to look at Joanna sitting in the seat reserved for witnesses before swivelling back to stare at me. But this is pure cliché, Denise; you can see that, can't you? Yes, I was for a short time 'involved' with Ms Sharpe, a pallid, wispy civil servant—younger, but not that much younger—who came into the shop from time to time. Not unattractive; slightly owlish, with spectacles, and a pointy chin. But it was never serious, so far as I was concerned; a match which briefly flared and then went out. I was careful to cover my tracks; Alice never once said anything to me, and I am certain she did not know. And even if I did tell Joanna I would leave Alice (which I cannot at this remove deny), so what? How many men involved in such a liaison have not made the same tawdry declaration in a moment of weakness, or ardour, or both? Anyway, our 'affair' — Hagan will relish the word — had ended before Alice disappeared, no matter what Joanna now maintains; her witness statement makes it clear I had not seen or spoken to her for almost two weeks before what happened.

You make an entry in your notepad and then turn the page.

Collins is still sulking at your reprimand. 'You could at least have *tried* to save her.'

I stare at him. 'You think she's dead, don't you? You're not listening to me.'

'Morris, please. We do need to explain what happened next.'

A nimble intervention, Denise; thank you.

Let me say that Alice had lost a lot of blood. I am not a doctor, but I could not see how she could survive even if I had managed to get her to a hospital. I realise how weak this sounds as an explanation; but isn't the implausibility itself more plausible than a neat, 'pat' answer? The incongruity seized on by the weary detective, the sense of something 'not quite right' which betrays the guilty party; these belong in fiction. Reality is different. Reality is littered with loose ends, bits unaccounted for, the strands and threads left over from the nets we've woven of our lives. If I was to lie, Denise, I'd have made up something believable; credit me that, at least. If I'd wanted to kill her, I could have sliced open her wrists and watched her die: I could then have played the distraught husband, wild-eyed with grief as the paramedics and the hospital workers tried desperately to save her. But I didn't.

And if I had managed to get her to a hospital, and if somehow she had lived? I would have had to tell them what she had done; the self-immersion, the incisions made to assist her breathing underwater — gills, in effect. Would they have understood what Alice had...become? I doubt it. They would have sedated her, and strapped her to a bed while they noted down the details of what would be described as her 'psychosis', and then they would have assembled the documents necessary to have her committed. I could not bear that, and nor could she. In our time together we had had The Discussion many times, about what we would do for each other if either of us became grievously and permanently incapacitated. No lolling in a wheelchair, no staring blankly out the window of some wretched nursing home, none of that. We relied on each other to ensure that our end, when it came, would be quick and painless. Though for Alice this was most certainly not 'the end'.

The blood kept oozing from the gashes she'd made in her ribcage; I tried to bandage them with towels, but she put her hand on mine to signal me to stop. I carried her to our bedroom and wrapped her in a bed sheet before bringing her downstairs and out to the car. Eventually I managed to open the back door and lift her in. She was moaning and wriggling on the seat, and I knew I didn't have much time. I drove down to the pier, lifted her out and carried her to the little slipway. It was still dark and the pier seemed deserted; I had not spotted the courting couple parked above on the high road so diligently tracked down by Willis, but, yes, they would have seen me heading towards the water, bearing my wife's almost lifeless body in my arms. The tide was in. I laid her down on the slipway, unwrapped the bed sheet, and looked at Alice for the last time.

And how, Denise, does one say goodbye? There are rituals, ceremonies, but there is no right way — and no wrong way — to part. It is in the end a matter of instinct, of pure *feel*. A generation ago, were I to be convicted of this crime, you would be here with me in Ravenstone on the morning of my execution, searching for the appropriate words to say before realising there are none, since what people want most at a leave-taking is not words but companionship; to feel they are not alone. Alice's eyes were clouding over; a mixture of pleading and sadness. She knew this was an act of mercy; she wanted it, I have no doubt. Yet she also knew — we both knew — that we would almost certainly never see each other again. I kissed her, and held her hand for one final wordless moment. Then I half-rolled, half-slid her body off the slipway and into the water.

What happened next is uncorroborated, I accept. Even the couple cavorting in the car have acknowledged to Willis that they could not see beyond the slip. As I looked down at my wife's body in the glittery darkness of the waves, Alice turned slowly onto her back and smiled up at me. Then she rolled onto her front, stretched her arms out to part the water, surged under the surface and away. Away from me, away from the slip; out into the bay. Gone. I stood at the edge a moment longer, wondering if I'd get one last glimpse of her. But no. The light was beginning to brighten in the east. I picked up the bed sheet—yes, yes, stained with Alice's blood—and returned to the car, where I stuffed it in the boot and drove home.

*

Once upon a time in a village in northern Spain named Lierganes there lived a widow and her four sons. They were very poor, and so the widow had no choice but to send one of her sons, Francisco (allow me, for the purposes of the story, Denise, to say he was her favourite) to Bilbao to work as a carpenter. He was red-haired, pale-skinned; a good worker too, and although he liked the city he never forgot the village that he came from, and his mother's house with bluebells by the door. One evening Francisco and two friends went swimming in the waters off Bilbao. He was a good swimmer, but the currents where the three rivers drain into the estuary are treacherous, and Francisco was quickly swept out to sea. Imagine the helpless shouting of his friends. Imagine as well the little party arriving at the widow's house and standing outside, afraid to knock; his tearful one-time companions who have made the journey from Bilbao, and a couple of women from the village who know the widow, and a priest. Her other sons sit with her as she weeps. All she can think of is the son who's lost to her forever, his milky skin and copper hair.

Years pass; five years, to be exact. In the bay of Cádiz, hundreds of miles to the south, the seas are rough; a fishing boat is pitching in the waves. There is something tangled in the nets, something big. The fishermen strain to haul their catch aboard and then step back, alarmed by the creature thrashing on the aft deck among the grouper-fish and pompano: it has a strip of scales down its back, and what look like gills on either side, but its shape and form are human, a young man, naked, with pale skin and red hair. The crew are afraid; this can only mean bad luck, so they turn back. Near the harbour in Cádiz there is a friary, and because the skipper is a God-fearing man, and anxious to rid his ship of any curse, the fishermen take the creature to the friary where it may be exorcised of evil. After days of frugal care, and probing questions from the mendicants, the creature utters a single word: 'Lierganes.' What does this mean, they wonder: who, or what is Lierganes? No one seems to know, until one evening in a bar down in the port a sailor from the north of Spain hears the story. Lierganes is a village near where I come from, he says, and five years ago a widow there lost her favourite son when he was drowned, a boy with red hair and pale skin. The fishermen are sceptical, but the head of the friary says: 'Let me take him north.' So they travel the length of Spain; by horse and cart, since this is the seventeenth century, and on the outskirts of the village the friar releases the creature from the ropes that tie him to the cart and says to those who have travelled with him: 'Let us see what he does next.' And what he does is truly remarkable, this fishman, this *hombre pez*: he leads them through the village, along streets he clearly knows until he arrives outside a house with bluebells at the door. 'Home,' he says, and when he knocks the door is answered by the widow. 'Francisco!' she cries.

Ningyo. Finfolk. Merrows. Selkies. There are many stories, Denise; too many to ignore. There's a certain logic to all this: if, as we are told, we all come from the sea in the first place, is there any reason why some of us might not feel compelled to go back? And there is something else: our willingness to accept the existence of another world, another life, a *next* life, is a comfort and a consolation, and the basis of almost every religion. This is more than just imagination. The urge to believe what seems otherwise unbelievable makes the dreadful world we live in bearable. You want the story of Francisco to be true because the widow's grief is so painful; you want to see her weeping tears of joy as she clasps her long-lost son. You, Denise, and Collins here—and the jury, especially the jury—what we all want, in the end, is to have our spirits raised by a story that might even be true, a happy-ever-after.

*

A tap on the door of the interview room; McCutcheon, anxious to clock off so as to feed his cavernous belly, is wondering how much longer we will be. Collins opens the door a crack. 'We just need five more minutes,' he says, resuming his seat as McCutcheon lumbers away. Collins looks at you. 'What about Dr Shaw?' he says, inclining his head in my direction. How dare you, sir; how dare you. But I must keep my temper; and so I confine myself to raising my hand quickly to silence his impudence. No psychiatrists, please. I will not allow some tweedy, well-meaning healthcare professional to try to explain away what happened by reference to some cheap theory of delusion. I'm better than that, Denise. *You're* better than that.

You rub your eyes and replace your glasses. Our time here is almost over. The next occasion on which we'll meet will be the first day of the trial. You will be all business in the sombre, panelled courtroom, lipsticked and briskly efficient, robed in your ancient ceremonial gown; in your element, one might say. Right now, though, you are tired. You close your papers with a sigh, your hands resting on top as you ask your final question.

'Is there anything else you want to say?'

Oh Denise: what do I need to do?

I smile at Collins. 'May I?' I say, as I take a sheet of paper from his notebook. His pen I take as well: a slim, elegant stylus of burnished gold — or is it? Gold, I mean?

This lustre, this brassy hue could be fool's gold, couldn't it? I place the sheet of paper in the middle of the table, in front of you, and I begin to write, upside-down, from my right to left across the page — a party-trick learned in St Thomas's during the long reaches of drizzly afternoons. The word slowly appears in front of you. When I am finished I nudge the piece of paper in your direction and smile. Then I reach across the table, and place my hand on yours.

A silence blooms briefly in the room's stale air before Collins, embarrassed by my transgression, begins noisily stuffing papers into his bag. To your credit, Denise, you do not flinch. Instead you return my smile with a half-smirk of your own. Am I imagining it, or is there a wistfulness, playing at the edges of your lips; is that *affection*? I wonder might things have been otherwise between us, you and me, if we had met in another world, another life? Perhaps. Then you look down at what I've written, and carefully you enunciate the word.

*

I've made it up. The name for it, I mean. I'm no Greek scholar—and no anthropologist either, for that matter— but I'm actually quite proud of it. You know that the 'ichthus' is a symbol consisting of two intersecting arcs, the right-side ends extending beyond the meeting point so as to suggest the shape of a fish? Fishers of men, is what Jesus promised to make of his apostles; and the fish shape was used widely as a symbol of Christianity—far less inflammatory than the cross, I'm sure you agree. In times of Christian persecution, a stranger meeting another on the road would draw one arc in the dirt; if his new companion drew the other, they could both relax, knowing they could trust each other. Isn't this what's happened here to us, Denise: our lives two intersecting arcs? I like to think so. I like to think as well that some day we may meet again on a road somewhere, where we will both bend down and trace two lines that come together in the dust.

And the word itself has a kind of resonance; the transformation of one into another. After all, this is what you do, Denise, isn't it? Shape-shifting, reordering the evidence, morphing and realigning, shuffling the facts until you have constructed the creation which you want the jury to believe in. Suppose, for a moment, I've made all of it up: the broken shell, the goodly doctor, the brimming bath and oozing wounds, and the tear-jerking finale as I held my wife for the last time beside the water's edge? What if, instead, Alice had simply found out about Joanna and, despite my pleas, had told me that evening that I would have to leave? What if I had become so enraged that I had killed her and then set about disposing of the body? How dreary such a squalid tale would be. You see, you should be grateful to me, Denise; I have given you something new, something utterly different to the catalogue of sordid criminal cases you appear in. Because, yes, my life has changed; but when this case opens and you begin your role as my defence counsel, your life will change as well. This is my gift to you: the trial of the decade, perhaps the trial of a lifetime, since in one sense the whole world will be your jury. Do you understand this, Denise? Because if I can make you believe me when I tell you what happened, then surely you can make them believe as well. All you need to do is trust me.

ACKNOWLEDGEMENTS

Grateful acknowledgements are due to the editors of the following who published or broadcast versions of some of the stories in this collection: *Books Ireland*; *Counterparts: A Synergy of Law and Literature* (The Stinging Fly Press); *Crannóg*; *The Gloss*; *The Hennessy Book of Irish Fiction 2005-2015* (New Island); *The Irish Times*; The Irish Writers Centre; RTE Radio *The Book On One*; *Stinging Fly*; *Sunday Independent*; and *Sunday Tribune*.

I wish also to thank various people who provided encouragement, help and advice to me during the making of these stories over the years: Sarah Bannan, Greg Baxter, Michael Bevan, David Browne, Neil Burkey, David Butler, Ciaran Carty, Zoe Comyns, DBC Writers, Martin Doyle, Catherine Dunne, Tanya Farrelly, Lisa Frank, Carlo Gebler, Anthony Glavin, Ashley Honeysett, everyone at the Irish Writers Centre, Cormac Kinsella, Jane McDonnell, Sarah McDonnell, Danielle McLaughlin, Siobhán Mannion, Declan Meade, Lia Mills, John Minihan, Marcella Morgan, Liz Nugent, Catherine O'Brien, the late Tom O'Dea, Vanessa Fox-O'Loughlin, Sean O'Reilly, Fiona O'Rourke, Kieran Ryan, everyone at Staccato Spoken Word Events, everyone at Some Blind Alleys, Bill Tinley, Dominique Tuohy, the late Caroline Walsh, John Walsh, Tríona Walsh, Yve Williams, Eilis Wren.

Special thanks to Michelene and to William, Jack, Eavan and Tom for keeping me afloat.

JOHN O'DONNELL's work has been published and broadcast widely in Ireland and abroad. Fiction publications include *Counterparts* (The Stinging Fly Press), *Hennessy Book of Irish Fiction, Sunday Tribune, Sunday Independent, The Stinging Fly, Books Ireland, The Irish Times*, and RTE's *The Book on One*. Awards include the Hennessy Award for Emerging Fiction and Cúirt Festival of Literature New Writing Prize for Fiction. He has also published four poetry collections, the latest of which is *Sunlight: New and Selected Poems* (Dedalus Press, 2018): prizes for poetry include the Irish National Poetry Prize, the Ireland Funds Prize and the Hennessy Award for Poetry. He lives and works in Dublin.